NECTAR OF AMBROSIA

A.L. HAWKE

PHANTOM HEART, LLC

ISBN: 978-1-953919-34-2 (paperback)

ISBN: 978-1-953919-35-9 (hardback)

ISBN: 978-1-953919-31-1 (ebook)

Library of Congress Control Number: 2023936855

This is a work of fiction. It all comes directly from the imagination of the author's mind. This includes names, characters, places, and incidents. Any public names are used solely for creative purposes. Any resemblance to actual people, living or dead, or to companies, institutions or locales is entirely coincidental or accidental.

Line edited by Stephanie Marshall Ward

Proofread by Alexa B., alexabooks.wixsite.com/authors

Cover © 2023 by Brosedesignz

Published by Phantom Heart, LLC

27702 Crown Valley Pkwy D-4, #201

Ladera Ranch, CA 92694, USA

Printed and bound in the United States of America

First printing May, 2023

Learn more about A.L. Hawke at www.alhawke.com

Correspondence: contact@alhawke.com

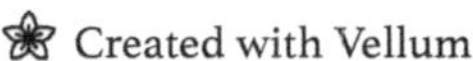 Created with Vellum

1

UNOSTENTATIOUS

I SNUCK INTO ASHER'S LECTURE. YEAH, IT'S FUN. NOT THE lecture, of course. The lecture's boring as hell—I mean, it's a midterm review about syntax and sentence structure. But, using the local vernacular, pretending to be a college student is *SICK*.

Ash and I are sitting two rows from the stage in a packed, windowless lecture hall with fold-up theater chairs and a large stage with peach walls. Onstage, a lady with long blond hair is walking stiffly by the podium, talking through a mic in her collar. She's talking all excitedly about how words are somehow similar to road signs. That's really funny. I couldn't care less. I just like being here and holding my boyfriend's hand under our armrest. *Sigh*. Well, you know by now that Medusa's a total romantic monster.

Asher leans by my ear and whispers, "Sorry it's so dull, Gorgi."

He gazes back at the stage, brushing back his long blond hair. Then he stiffens. Because his professor is standing before us watching him talk to me during her review lecture. Asher told me this professor wants all her students totally quiet. I get it. Sometimes students get rowdy in my library too. When students get rambunctious with me, I also shush them. If they don't listen, I let them have a quick glimpse of my golden eyes. And if that doesn't stop the yapping, my eyes turn green and I show a stray slithering friend.

"It's not boring," I whisper to Ash as the lecturer turns away. I reposition my thick glasses over my eyes. "I love it."

Okay, it's total Snoozeville. I've entertained the idea of going to one of his classes all year, only they're in the morning. I can't do mornings. Those wigglies in my hair, my snakes, go crazy in sunlight.

"We'll have more fun later," I whisper in his ear.

He squeezes my hand tightly over that, which I love. I look at Ash's profile again. His blond hair. His chiseled cheekbones. His stubble and his—see it? He's smiling 'cause he knows I'm looking. God, I love him.

Is this what living life is all about? Finding that right man that you go head over heels over? It almost takes one's mind off being a fearsome, snake-haired, fanged creature of the night.

Says you, Gorgiana. I like my hair.

Yeah, says me, Medusa. Now, shh... Let's enjoy Ash playing with my fingers.

Yeah. That's nice.

But Asher loses his smile. So does the professor. And this time, it's not over us yapping. The lecturer furrows her brow, staring at something on the right side of the lecture hall.

"Uh-oh," Asher says.

Everyone's looking over. I don't. I don't need to. I can smell their stench. But my hair's practically pulling itself out of my bun, pulling my head in their direction. Three men wearing pitch-black suits and shades are quietly moseying down a side aisle, coming to kill us.

Get Asher out of here!

I know. I know.

My phone buzzes. It's loud enough to get everyone's attention, including the professor. She stares right at me from the stage.

"Sorry," I mutter. I look down at my phone. *Aner*. I'd recognize that contact anywhere. But I haven't seen his texts for nearly a year now.

Aner is the code name for that god Hades. He's the head of all sorts of secret spy stuff in the USA. His code name is Orcus, which means death. Like killer whales. Orca. And he supposedly protects me and Ash, not because he cares about me—he does everything for my best friend, his favorite goddess: Cora, the goddess Persephone. Anyway, just seeing his name on my phone makes me shudder because it means we're in trouble.

Get Asher the fuck out of here, Gorgi!

Aner texts only one word: *Imada*.

The three bad guys are looking at me, but even with their shades, they turn away from me to avoid my cursed eyes. My phone buzzes again.

"Please, all cellphones need to be turned off," says the professor.

"Sorry."

I peek down. *"Return home. NOW."*

Ash slowly rises and steps around my legs, heading away from the goons. Then I get up and move around another ton of legs. Of course, the bad guys are right behind us, but they're walking slowly while the professor continues lecturing.

It's all I can do to not break through the doors, carry Ash, and make a run for it. But then I cover my eyes. They've probably changed from golden yellow to shiny emerald. And my hair's breaking its tie ready to turn full-on viper-mode, ready to snap back, wrap around their necks, and fucking squeeze the life out of them.

When we get outside, it's dark. Lights shine over the walkways between buildings. Ash grabs my hand again, this time walking faster. I smell them exiting right behind us.

I do what I never do. I call *Aner* on my cellphone. It rings and rings and rings as we break into a run, holding hands. And rings. And rings...

"*Never* call me on this number, Medusa."

"They're right behind us!" I turn and they quickly avert their eyes.

"*Discreetly* lose them. Unostentatiously. No dismembered limbs. Lose them. You're on your own, Medusa."

"Ask him what they want," says Ash.

"What the hell do they want?" I ask. But he hung up. Because the god of the Underworld is a total asshole. I angrily stuff the phone back in my pants pocket.

"Your hair, Gorge," Ash says.

Yep, snakes are hissing all over the place. The hair tie's long gone.

You've gotta get Asher to safety!

I know, Medusa, I know.

When we're between two buildings, I yank Ash's hand hard. He gasps as we slide straight down a hill. I don't think he expected me to randomly jump through the bushes along the hillside. I didn't either. It's steep and I have to be careful. As it just rained, we're sliding on wet leaves and mud. But I know a place to hide.

Don't hide. Lead them to me. I'll tear their muscle from sinew—

But one shot—

Fucking turn around and let me at 'em!

Midway down the hill, I obey my more aggressive half. I turn. It's dark, but my green eyes are now glowing shiny emerald, lighting up the hillside. I have to cover them with my hands.

"Do you see them, Ash?" I sniff around.

"No."

"God, Ash," I say in a hushed voice, "we've gotta get you home."

"Why do you think they're after us again?"

"I don't know."

"Can you call Cora?"

"She said not to. She said something bad's coming down. Now I see that." I shake my head, still covering my eyes to keep us hidden. Then I repeat what the jerk said. "We're on our own."

"Let's run back to the main road. We're not far from your house."

"Shh, not yet," I whisper. "They're right above us on the hill. I smell them. I think they know we ran down here."

I can't look because then my green beacon would shine again. But I smell everything. I see a green schemata map as my nose reveals their positions.

After the three disperse, I feel a chill. One of them is lying on his stomach positioning a rifle aimed in our direction. He's looking through a scope. I grab Ash and break into a run again, but not further up the hill, as Medusa is telling me to do. I head toward the swamp at the bottom of the hill.

"Medusa. Medusa. Stop or we'll shoot him."

HIM, GORGI? Did you hear that! He said HIM!

I throw Ash to the ground. Then I cover his body with mine.

"What do you want!" I cry.

"Just a word."

"You came to capture me?"

"We're looking for the Mandrigel. Where's the Mandrigel?"

"What's a Mandrigel?"

"Don't act stupid, Medusa. Where are you hiding the Mandrigel?"

I'm doing everything I can to cover every inch of Asher's body. If the bullets fly, they'll hit my cursed immortal body, not him. See, I can take bullets. He can't. But he's taller than me. I've tried to gather him up in a ball, but I can't cover everything, so I keep trying to shield him. He's digging himself into the ivy and mud. I'm so nervous; he's moaning and struggling to breathe under my weight. But he's not objecting. I think he knows exactly what I'm doing.

"Tell us where he is or we'll fire."

"I don't know where he is! Okay?" I growl like a lion. "I don't even know what the hell you're talking about! Leave us alone!"

My rage is uncontrollable. Ash moans again from my pressing too hard against his chest.

"The spider woman told him to find you in Sunland, Florida," he replies. "The spider said you'd be in Sunland. The Mandrigel came for you. That means he's here. I'll give you twenty seconds to 'fess up his exact location, Medusa. Then we open fire."

"You fire and you die!"

I hear Ash's heart. It's vibrating rapidly like a bird. I fight with myself to avoid letting him go. You know, half of me wants to race up the hillside, grab the sniper, and snap his body in half.

"Ten seconds."

"I don't know, okay!" I cry. "I don't even know what you're talking about!"

"Time's up."

Crack.

It's muffled. Then another shot. And then another. I clutch Ash so tightly. It's gunfire, but the sound is tempered by a silencer. I've pulled Ash's body into a ball so tight that he groans again. Two more shots. I clutch him, but then I realize nothing's hitting us. Not one bullet has hit a leaf or branch around us.

My snakes snap back and scan the hillside. All three bodies are lying on the ground motionless. They're not holding their weapons. They've fallen with outstretched arms—dead.

I let go of Ash. He takes a deep breath. Then I jump up in fury, full of adrenaline, ready to scale the hill.

"Stop hiding, Medusa," whispers a different voice. "Come up the hill." I'd recognize that voice anywhere. It's Hades. "Your backup has arrived."

"Great timing, motherfucker! Asher almost got shot."

Asher grabs my arm and says softly, "He saved us, Gorgi. I'm fine. Everything's fine."

"It's not." I hug Ash. "Oh God, it's not okay. I'm so sorry. I'm so sorry, Ash."

"Stop the sentimentalities," the jerk says. "Come up the hill. I'll debrief you."

"I hate you!" I snap, looking back up the hill. It's said with more venom than I intended. But, you know, my adrenaline is on super overdrive. I feel my hair move in his direction and hiss at him.

"Inconsequential. Come up the hillside. You two are safe now, Medusa."

2

HOPE

WHEN ASHER AND I OPEN THE FRONT DOOR TO MY HOME, I sniff in every direction. My snakes are scanning the living room, kitchen, hallway, bathroom, and bedroom in my small house. Then I look around the backyard. When the coast is clear, I cry. Not yell or scream or growl like a beast. I mean I am fucking bawling my eyes out. Yeah, right inside the threshold of my door I cry and cry like a stupid whiny baby. Because you know the fearsome viper-haired monster Medusa is really just a crybaby.

Asher puts his arms around me.

"God, all it would have taken is one stray bullet, Ash. You should leave me. Just go away from me."

"It's *our* trouble, Gorge," Ash says, squeezing me tighter and kissing my forehead.

"They're not after you, they're after me," I say, shaking my head. "If something happens to you, Ash, I'll never forgive myself. You have to leave me."

"Gorgi," he says quietly. "Stop it. We're together on everything. Remember?"

I lean back a little and push the hair from my eyes. Of

course, one of the strands is a slimy wiggly. My hair's hissing snakes because I'm still worked up. But, Ash, well Ash, he doesn't care. He avoids my gaze though. My stupid green eyes are lighting up the dark house.

"I guess you can stay with me if you want to be crazy like that."

He gently pushes my hair from my forehead. I'm wondering if it's a wiggly. "I love you," he says. And he gently kisses my lips.

"Sure, crazy." I lean my forehead into his chest. Then he lets go of me. He switches on a light and heads to the adjoining kitchen.

"You know why they're after us?" he asks.

"Have no idea."

He takes a Saran-wrapped roast he made a day ago from the fridge. He unwraps it and throws it on a metal tray and puts it into the oven. Then he reaches for a bottle of red wine from our pantry.

"What are you doing?" I ask.

"Warming up food. Aren't you hungry? Don't think you and I are going out tonight. Anyway, cooking takes my mind off things."

I sit down at our round dining table and plop my head in my hands, running my fingers through my long hair, feeling sorry for myself. A few wigglies move and that only makes me feel worse.

"They mentioned Arachne," he says, turning on a light in the oven and watching his roast re-warm. "The *spider woman*, they said?"

"Yeah. I'm so worried about her, you don't even know."

He hands me some red wine. I sip some. It's good. Smooth. Then he's back to staring into the oven. He taps the glass in the oven window and cocks his head back.

"Feeling better?"

"No."

"Did Hades say if there were any more of those agents in town?"

"He doesn't know."

Ash comes over to my chair, leans down, and kisses my cheek. "We're fine, Gorgi."

He intends to head back to the kitchen—but not before I snatch his T-shirt. I pull him toward me and plop my lips on his. Then we smooch. And then we totally make out. Is it because we're in danger? Yeah, probably. You know, my Medusa-mode doesn't only make me turn violent, it turns me on. All that animalistic fervor comes out, and I want to take him, tear off his shirt, pants, and underwear, and fuck him right on the kitchen table.

"Gorge—" He laughs. "Gorge."

"Hmm?"

"Not now, babe."

His shirt somehow came off and my eyes, even in the yellow light of my house, brighten his pecs and ab muscles, turning his tanned skin a shade of green.

But the stove alarm dings.

"Got to get our food," he says.

"No, stay here."

He shakes his head and I'm forced to let him go. He brings over the roast. It's sizzling. So is his yummy naked chest. He cuts two slices for my plate.

"Sorry, no time to make any sides," he says.

The meat is delicious, even left over from a few days ago. Asher is a really good cook. Especially at the barbeque. And maybe the few days it marinated in the tray made it taste even better? I sip some red wine and look over at my man across the table. By habit, he quickly averts his eyes. But he smiles.

"Feeling better?"

"No, I'm not, Ash." And my head's back in my hands. "I was starting to like things being calm. You know, not having to run from agents in sunglasses."

He shrugs. "Can I have my shirt back?"

"No."

I cut more meat and fork it into my mouth. That's when there's a knock at the door. I hear a man's voice. I cringe. I'd recognize that bastard god's voice anywhere.

"May I come in?"

"*No!*"

He actually chuckles. Then he's laughing as he breaks into my house. He has no difficulty coming through the door, of course. He probably has a spare key. Hell, he's fixed my place twice after it was wrecked by Imada violence over the past year. He never asked my permission to do that either.

He walks inside and hangs a long black coat on a hanger by the door. It's wet. It must be raining. He's wearing all black; only his bald head is shining in the light from the kitchen. He's such a tall, broad-shouldered brute.

"Didn't Kore warn you they'd be coming?" Hades asks.

"She warned me by telling me I couldn't call. I texted her that everything'd be fine as long as she didn't bring Grace."

"She brought me instead."

"I should have mentioned you."

He gives me a stupid smirk. God, I hate him. But Ash, being the amazingly nice guy he is, actually gestures to an empty seat at our table. He put his shirt back on too—that's too bad. Then the god of the Underworld actually walks over and sits down beside my boyfriend at our small table. Sitting, he's almost as tall as Asher standing. Our uninvited guest looks at the wine bottle on the counter. He jumps up, grabs it for himself, and takes a wine glass from a line of them on the nearby counter. Then he pours himself a glass. Ash actually grabs a plate for him.

"He's not invited," I say.

Hades looks at Asher.

"It's her house," Ash says with a shrug.

Hades looks at his glass of wine. He lifts it above his head, swirls it a bit, and then sips some more as if he's taste testing a forty-year-old delicacy specially shipped from France. It's a red blend. A very good blend, actually, that I got at Trader Joes. He shakes his head and wrinkles his nose. Well, I guess it's not good enough for his uppity self—like I care. Then he infernally takes a fork and knife and pulls the whole roast toward him. That pisses me off enough to open a drawer, grab a meat cleaver, walk over to the table, and sever a huge juicy chunk for the fucker.

Hades chuckles.

Ash slowly eats, but he keeps glancing at me. I've got my arms folded, standing over Hades and staring at him.

"I saved this human's life, Medusa," Hades says with his mouth full of meat, pointing at Ash. "I'd think that deserves a word tonight."

"How do I know you didn't bring them here as another trap?"

"And then kill them? That would be a strange thing to do. Sit. Sit and I'll give you your debriefing. We're family, after all."

"Don't ever say that."

"I heard them asking for the Mandrigel," Ash says. "What's a Mandrigel?"

"Indeed, human. I've come to explain." He lifts a finger with his sardonic, devilish grin. But before he speaks, he chews more meat. "I must say, I'm flabbergasted. I didn't know you could cook, Medusa."

"It's leftovers," I say. "And I didn't. Asher made it."

Hades puts his fork and knife down and stares at Ash. He grows a really big smile. "You made this, sir?"

That does it. I can't stand another second of him. Now, with that smirk, I know he's insulting Ash. I rush over and yank at his arm. I'm ready to toss him out. I'm so hyped up from the fight that I'm ready to battle him to get him out of the house.

"Look, either say what you're going to say or leave. But don't insult him. Why don't you text me your debriefing and get the hell out."

"Gorgi!" Asher objects.

I yank again. If he were human, it would have tossed him five feet in the air. But he's a god. And as an infernal god, he is—of course—like ten times stronger than me. He furrows his brow and just stares at my hand. My fingernails have grown sharp, because I'm so pissed, but even their sharpness doesn't affect his skin.

"What are you doing?" he asks, amused. "Unhand your guest, please, so that he may try some more of your man's delicious meat."

"I said, go!" I let go of him. But then a snake in my hair darts past his face and pecks at it. Its fangs cut a deep gash in his cheek...

Oops.

"Sorry," I mutter.

Hades holds his cheek. Blood trickles down his fingers. Then his eyes open wide and flash fiery red. He scoots his chair back and flicks his wrist toward me. Some invisible force launches my whole body into the living room. I land face-first on the carpet.

"You wish a fight!" he cries. "Is that it, Gorgon?"

"Sir, you insulted us first," Ash says.

He whirls around and glares at Asher. I've been thrown

across the house, but I still smell the two of them by the table.

"I won't leave until I've debriefed her," thunders Hades. "The rat's surely coming, if he hasn't already, and she needs to be informed. This is business not pleasure. Just as she can't stand me, I don't wish to stay in her snake pit any longer than necessary."

I've had enough. I fold my arms and just sit on the couch, alone, in the adjoining living room.

After a minute, I hear their silverware clanging against their plates. That beast is actually eating dinner with my boyfriend.

Let me strike his face again, Gorgi. Pleeease.

That bite was a bit much.

"What's a Mandrigel?" Ash asks again.

"A Mandrigel is a slave, human," Hades says with his mouth full. His tone has become completely civil again. Because he's a two-faced bastard. "A Napean dwarf. A race that once thrived in the drowned kingdom of Azure Blue. Once there was a whole litter of rats living in their hovels beneath Mount Olympus. First, they mined the earth for gold. Later, some settled above ground on the island of Napea to serve my brother Poseidon. Then with the rise of my beloved Amazon nymph queen, Harmonia, they were all left underground stoking the flames that provided energy for my realm and the Mount."

"Will you return to the table, Medusa?" he hollers. "I didn't come to debrief your man-friend, I came to debrief you."

I don't say a word.

"Not bad meat, sir," Hades says to Ash. Disgustingly, his mouth is full. "You misunderstood me. I was once a king. In that time, women were not like the women of today. Back then, a man would never cook. Men fought. It was a far better time."

"Because you're a misogynist prick," I snap.

"Hardly." Hades chuckles. "I led women to conquer men. Anyway, Medusa, you can obviously hear us, so I shall continue my debriefing.

"After the Amazon nymphs chased the Mandrigel into the ground, Azure Blue was left free to be ruled by nymphs, a race my deluded wife Persephone believes she belongs to. Of course, Cora was actually born to the goddess Demeter, or Sara. But my wife's confused. She believes her mother to be Queen Nephrea. And so she thinks her girl and her lover, Gabriel, are part of her family. That is why she protects her lover and—"

"Her *husband*, Gabriel," I correct him.

"Her *lover*, Gabriel, and her daughter Moros. They are family to her. The last of her Ambrosia family—unless you count my deluded wife."

"Cora isn't your wife anymore," I object again, still hollering from the other room. "She'd rather be dead than still be considered married to you. Why don't you get to the point so you can get the fuck out of my house."

He doesn't respond. I hear him chewing and chomping meat and sipping more wine. So I jump off the couch and walk over.

"Finish your debriefing and leave," I insist, standing over the kitchen table.

"Ah, the fearsome, famed monster graces us with her presence once more." Hades says with a chuckle, rubbing his eyes. "Aside from your hair, you are still the most lovely lady there ever was, Medusa."

"*Debrief* me and scram."

"With the destruction of Atlantis, Cora nearly destroyed her nymphs. But not only the nymphs, nearly every

Mandrigel dwarf." He raises a finger. "Except one: Engel." Hades's glass is empty. So he gets up and pours himself more. "Won't you sit down, Medusa? My cheek is nearly healed."

I lean back against the kitchen counter. Ash, the angel he is, actually gestures for me to sit. I quickly shake my head.

"We didn't know he was still alive until your pet spider, Arachne, spilled the beans in Italy," Hades says. "Arachne was captured on the shore of Santa Margherita." He raises a hand. "Don't worry. We got her out with my operatives. But before Arachne was freed, she 'fessed all about Engel. She said that he had lived with her in those underwater dens under San Fruttuoso for a century—before Imada destroyed the caves. But what is far more important to Imada is what this last Mandrigel possesses."

Then he stops. Yeah, typical of him—he goes through this whole drawn-out story and then just stops. Instead of finishing, he raises his wine glass and stirs the wine before his eyes again. He smells it and—

"What!" I snap, leaning forward. "What does Engel hold! Won't you get to the point!"

"He holds an elixir reminiscent of this wine." He swirls it again. "A possession so dear to one's palate. But a possession not fit for a human tongue. No. So great, it's not even fit for a god's."

He drinks from his glass.

"Won't you just say it!"

"Gorgi, calm down," Ash urges. "You're still changed."

I glance at Ash. He looks away. Then I sigh and cover my eyes with my hands. Ash is right, of course, as always. I'm still riled up from the fight. I can't get that hilltop off my mind. I keep seeing them lying down and aiming rifles at him.

"Just tell us and leave us alone, Hades," I say, running my hands through my hair and heaving a long sigh.

"Pandora's Box," Hades says. "That's it. The Jar of Pandora. Everyone wants it, including you."

Asher looks at me because he doesn't know what the hell Hades is talking about. But I don't know what the hell he's talking about either.

"You've never heard of Pandora?" Hades asks incredulously.

"I've heard of Pandora's Box," I say.

"Certainly, from spending endless hours in your library, you've read about Pandora, Medusa. But Pandora lived even before your time. I knew her personally. Prometheus brought man fire. His sister, Pandora, brought man plague. All from me." And he pompously taps his chest. "If you recall your mythology, Pandora, like the Christian Eve, was the first woman of our world. This is a myth, of course. Pandora was not the first female, but her treasure did open humans to disease. And she didn't bring pestilence only to Epimetheus's kingdom, she brought it to the world. Legend says that the box—a misnomer, it's a crystal jar—still held something when it was shut. Do you two know what that was?"

"Hope," says Ash.

"Bravo, human. Hope. How on Earth did you know that?"

"I've become very fond of Greek mythology lately," Asher says, winking at me.

"At your peril, child."

"You can't help but insult him!" I snap.

"Perhaps I wouldn't be so rude, Medusa, if you sat down with your guest."

"You're an uninvited guest." And I keep standing.

"Why would you give us disease?" asks Asher.

"It is symbolic, human. I didn't. I let loose knowledge, the greatest illness any feral mind can have. That is thought of as a gift. It is actually a sickness that is the source of all your misery."

"What about what's left in Pandora's Jar?" I ask.

"Yes, do you know what the actual substance in the jar was? This 'hope'? Can you guess it?" He swirls the red wine in his glass, stupidly raising it above his head. "Nectar. Nectar of the gods. The last remaining drops. Once it flowed like a waterfall in the forests of Mount Olympus—before my lovely Kore, Persephone, destroyed everything. Now the world holds only drops of it in a crystal jar. My entire family of gods wants it—even if there's only a drop left. Imada would kill for the power to make humans immortal. With nectar can be made ambrosia. And ambrosia can impart immortality to any mortal who tastes it. It means eternal life.

"Legend says that it was ambrosia that made the gods of my family immortal. The original nymph family and the Mandrigel dwarfs were also given ambrosia. Of course, they were given only a taste and are not immortal like the gods. But it magically turns them youthful. Persephone gave some to Nephrea as a gift, and she grew a half century younger. The nectar alone is poisonous. But when baked into ambrosia, it can be consumed. I even christened Harmonia's descendants 'Ambrosia.' That was our way of saying that her Amazon nymphs shall prosper forever.

"Now Imada wants these last remaining drops of nectar. Your enemies are hunting for it. We thought it had been lost. Now many are willing to end the world to get it."

"End the world for it?" Asher asks. "Why?"

Hades finishes his glass of wine and drops it on the table, nearly shattering the glass stem. He stares incredulously at Asher as if he's a moron.

"Such power could give your slithery girlfriend the

ability to impart a century or two more of life on you, sir. What mortal wouldn't want that? Even the monster you sleep with desires it. It's rather lonely living an eternity alone. Ask dowager lady Medusa."

"Where is the jar now?" Ash asks.

"With Engel. The question is, where is Engel?"

"Why not just destroy it?" I ask.

"You can't. The magical elixir must be prepared as ambrosia and then ingested. You can't blow the liquid up. And you can't burn it. Nor can you destroy the crystal container it lies in. You could bury it, but that would be stupid. Someone would find it. And they'd search. Believe me. So many have searched the bottom of the sea for the legendary world of Atlantis. Many thought it was to make an archeological discovery of a lost world. No. We know Atlantis existed. Archeologists aren't diving for ancient ruins, they're searching for nectar. No one has found a single drop under the sea. Diluted in the water? Maybe? But all of it is lost, except for the contents of this one jar. So this jar is the most valuable thing in the world. The jar contains, literally, drops from the fountain of youth."

He stands up.

"And now, you'll be thrilled to know that I've finished your debriefing. I shall take my leave." Then he looks right into my eyes—something no one ever does. "But before I go, I have two questions for you, Gorgon. Do you still have the Scepter of Azure?"

I nod.

"Guard it." He walks to the door. "I disagreed strongly with Kore for letting you have it. As Imada searches for the jar, they will not mind getting their hands on the Scepter of Azure either."

He touches the doorknob and adds, with a smirk, before leaving, "Oh, one last thing... Where is he?" He squints into my eyes, scrutinizing me. "Engel's a wily rat. He has lived thousands of years avoiding nearly all troubles by simply existing in the same boring way as you. He's perfected the ability to hide himself. You can't blame him. Imagine a blue-skinned dwarf the height of your waist trying to buy groceries in the local market. So I'm not sure you'd tell me where he is. He also has a way of convincing people to keep his presence a secret.

"And he detests me. I wasn't kind to his people when they served me in the Underworld. When the little man shows up, text *Aner*. No calls. I need that jar. You can have the blue dwarf, but I need the jar. Hope, you know, can be a dreadful thing when it is lost from our world."

3

COULD RAIN

ASHER DROPS ME OFF AT THIS BAR AND GRILL ON THE outskirts of town called The Cookie Cutter. It's a cute restaurant featuring these huge freshly baked cookies, dripping with frosting, that you can drool over behind glass counters while waiting for your table. All the waiters and waitresses wear these really cute white chef uniforms. And there's a string of large booths with tall seats, providing privacy from everybody in the place, which Ash and I love—'cause it gives me quiet time with him. I'm a private girl, you know. And, confidentially, totally a romantic, as you know. Anyway, Ash and I totally love this place. But tonight, I'm dreading it. Because I'm here to meet with Asher's sister. Sandra and I have never gotten along.

"I'm looking for Sandra," I say quietly to the maître d', shaking out the water from my umbrella. The maître d' is behind a desk across from the cookies. She ignores me, staring at her computer monitor.

Speak up, Gorgi!

I push a wiggly from my brow. I know they get riled up over being ignored.

"Can you show me the table reserved under the name Sandra?" I repeat more loudly.

The maître d' looks up. She's a tall young woman with short brown hair. I quickly avert my gaze from her and look at a cookie with blueberry frosting. Yum, it looks so good.

"Come right this way."

She walks me down a row of booths. It's kinda empty because it's only five thirty p.m. We turn the corner and meander down a row of tall booths. And then, behold... *The Bitch.*

Ash's sister is wearing snooty clothes, of course, including a swanky blouse. Her face is caked in makeup, and blond highlights streak her long, dark hair. The table is near the outdoor patio, and I can hear the rain hitting the windows. She's drinking a martini and staring at her phone. Her martini is clear, not in the style of my fun friend Cora. Cora's into red pomegranate martinis. I mean, Cora's the goddess Persephone, and you know Persephone loves pomegranates. But somehow, Persephone always drinks her cocktails in such a non-snooty way. It's like she is making fun of being snooty. Not Sandra. Sandra is full-on hoity toity parvenu.

"Gorgi," Sandra says with a fake grin. She looks right at my golden eyes—'cause she can, for a little while, anyway, as a woman.

Turn her to stone. Just do it!

Shh... Quiet, Medusa. We're not here for her. We're here for Ash.

Sandra frowns at my outfit and my thick goggle glasses, of course.

"It's so wet outside," I say, sitting down, really just to say something. "I almost slipped by the front door."

"That's not surprising," she mutters real quietly, raising an eyebrow. "I'm glad you didn't hurt yourself."

I sit down across from her. The booth can seat six people, so it's really big. That suits me. It gives me distance. I nod with a fake grin of my own. Then I shake out my hair, flinging some of the water from one of my snakes at her face. Did you do that on purpose?

Yep.

She flicks water off her cheek with disgust.

"Sorry I'm late," I add, heaving a sigh. "Ash came back from lecture later than he expected." She wanted to meet at five, but it's sunny at five, you know.

"And you can't drive," Sandra says. "Why is that anyway, Gorgiana?"

I furrow my brow and just glare at her.

"Forget it," she says, waving a hand dismissively.

She takes out a binder from under the booth. She opens it on the table, scooting a bit closer to me. She runs her finger down some photos of this place she's planning as her wedding venue. The pictures are stunning. I chose this really cool villa all decked out in Italian architecture over-looking the hills. I don't know, I guess Portofino, Italy, gave me some inspiration. She looks up all dreamy and smiles at me—like a real smile. "You sure you and Ash can pay for all this? This is so nice."

"I want to."

Of course Sandra, who's finally showing a glimmer of respect—something she never does—adores the gift. I lied and told her my parents have loads of money. Well, they passed a long time ago. But I'm rich. My riches are really from gathering odds and ends and selling antiques over the centuries.

Dad didn't even have much money as a carpenter in Sarpedon three thousand years ago.

"Look here at the patio," she says, pointing at the veranda in the photo. It's surrounded by Tuscan architecture. "Oh, I want to get pictures right here at one to two o'clock with Jack. It's so pretty. It's going to be amazing under the sun. I love that photographer you emailed me. There will be a taste testing in one week, on Sunday. And I want you and Ash to be there even a bit earlier to help set things up. And then we'll need to proceed with rehearsals the week of the wedding. I can't believe how fast it's approaching."

"I thought we agreed on pictures at sunset?"

"The best lighting is under sunlight, Gorgi. You know that. I mean, I was thinking we'd take pictures also at sunset. It's going to be so beautiful."

"The lights will be very pretty at night," I suggest.

She shakes her head. I give up. Of course, I know photos are better under sunlight, but I can't do pictures with her family under the sun. My wigglies will be in a tizzy at that time. Then again, I have to make an excuse to not be shown in photos, period. Do you know what happens when people stumble on pictures of me from decades ago? How about one to two centuries? I don't look a whole lot different.

"Sunlight always gives the best pictures, Gorgi," she says dismissively, turning the pages and looking at other outside views of the grounds. Then she laughs. "Ooh, just look at this hillside. I know it'll be the perfect place to showcase Jack's white suit and cute dimples."

For a second she looks up, dreamy about her fiancé. Or the grounds? I don't know. She laughs again. Then she looks at me and her grin vanishes.

"Afternoon," I grunt.

"Aha. One or two o'clock. Now here—" She claps her hands and gets all giddy. "Ooh, I want those tiny little lights all strung up in the air like this too! Doesn't that look gorgeous, Gorgi! With the tables on the grass, it's going to be so perfect. You know, Jack's parents love Italy. They were in Tuscany four years ago."

"Ash and I were in Portofino a few months ago."

"Jack's parents said that the views in the hills were to die for. And with these stone buildings with terracotta roofs and stone walkways, ooh, it should be so nice. Maybe we can get Italian food too? Like pizza?"

"Pizza's more American."

She looks at me, acting like she's recalling that she's sitting beside someone. "Yes, we should talk about the food."

"Yes," says a waitress, chuckling, near our table. "Are you two ready to order now? Would you like another martini?"

"Sure. And…" She looks at me. "Hey, what do you want, Gorge? Have you had the chance to see the menu?"

"Ash and I are regulars here. I don't need to see it." I turn to the waitress but look down.

"What would you like?" the waitress asks me.

"A Coke."

The waitress nods. I catch Sandra smirking at me.

What's so funny?!

"And I'll have your club sandwich and fries," I add.

"I'll have the salmon," Sandra says. "And, actually, instead of another martini, get me a glass of your house white wine. Your best pinot."

The waitress nods. "And I'll get you two some bread."

"I hope there's enough room on the grass for all our guests," she says, turning back to her binder. She turns a few more pages, looking at the grass field. "They say there's a two-hundred-and-fifty person limit here. I mean, Ash has a few buddies. I know his kinda nerdy friend Keith will be there for sure, but not sure about how many others. At least you don't really have anyone." She chuckles.

BITCH! Let me suck a fucking eye out of a socket right now!

She runs a hand along my forearm and says with a

smirk, "What about your mom? Your dad? I mean, your family, what of them, Gorgi? If they're shelling out so much money, you should invite anyone you want. Your whole family can come."

She actually thinks she's being nice, I think. And she's also thinking my family isn't large. Because I'm shy little Gorgiana. Right? She's so mean.

"This is your and Jack's special day," I say. "Anyway, my folks aren't into crowds." Of course, she believes that.

"Yes, let's move on to food." And she turns the pages of a menu. "Oh, see, they have pizza! They have pizza, Gorgi. That's perfect! Jack and I love pizza." Then she furrows her brow for a moment. At that moment the waitress hands us our drinks and some bread. She sips her wine, completely ignoring the waitress and then says quietly, still staring at the binder, "Is there a limit on the food?"

"Sky's the limit. But they also have wedding planners you can hire, you know, Sandra. I could arrange that."

"Oh, no," she says. She sips more wine. "That would be expensive."

"Well, I don't make much of a wedding planner."

"I know you don't. So looking here, hey, look, they have fries dipped in a sauce served on metal trays for appetizers. That is so sick! Or maybe we can get those mini hotdogs."

Well, that's one thing Sandra and I have in common. I absolutely love pigs in a blanket.

That's like the only thing you have in common.

"Is there anything *you* want, Gorgiana?" she asks again.

There's something about her trying to act nice that's worse than if she just completely ignored me. Still, she won't let up; she's staring at me. So I glance over. There's a page with elegant Indian naan with a tray of sauces that looks really good. "How about—"

"Should we serve people the pizza or do it buffet style?" she interrupts.

"Serving is more elegant."

"Yeah, especially if we're gonna do pizza. But... I want all these different selections for our guests. I want them to try whatever they want. So I think they'll have to get up to choose the kind of pizza slices they want. Doesn't that sound cool?"

She makes me smile. I must admit, I kinda love that Sandra loves pizza. You know, as much as I absolutely detest her, the fact that her snooty eyes go right to pizza for her wedding is very Asher-like.

I like pizza.

I know, Medusa. We fucking love pizza. And so does Asher's bitch sister. Maybe she's not so bad?

"Well, if you're going to go with pizza, maybe go with a flatbread style," I suggest. "That's more authentically Italian."

"No," she says finally, pulling her eyes from the menu. She turns to me and I look away. "I want these. Look at all the different meats we can add. Let's do this. Yes. I want pizza just like this for my wedding."

"American pizza." I can't help but turn from her and roll my eyes.

"No, pizza like this," she objects. "It's perfect for our little Italy. God, Gorgi..." She makes me jump as she throws an arm around me. "Please thank your folks for doing this! It's going to be so much fun!"

I nod. Then I try to recover from the shock of her hugging me.

"But...what should we do about drinks?" she asks.

"How about an open bar?"

She opens her eyes wide and nods slowly. "How can your parents afford all this? What do your parents do?"

"Dad's a carpenter."

"Well, I'm going to be so grateful to you and Ash. I'd like you to be one of my bridesmaids."

"Really, Sandra?"

"Of course. You're Ash's girlfriend."

"Thanks, Sandra."

"Great!" And she hugs me again. I jump again. She's never hugged me before in my life. "It's going to be so amazing."

"Well…" I turn to the window facing the patio. "It could rain."

She loses her smile. She slowly looks over my shoulder at the window. Of course, though it's dark, we can hear water dripping outside and the rain pelting the patio.

I suppose that was mean.

That was brilliant! Ha, ha! That was A LOT mean.

As our waitress comes over with our meal, Sandra can't help continuing to look out the window.

"Thank you, Gorgiana," Sandra says quietly, closing the binder. Then she just sips from her wine glass.

"Oh, just thank Ash."

I hate myself for mentioning the weather. But it could rain and, if it does, I think my alternate venue, inside one of the small conference halls, is going to seriously suck. Then Sandra will just attribute everything sucking to silly, sad Gorgiana. But even though I really hate her, I really regret saying that. All of Sandra's excitement and happiness seems to have left her.

It's really weird, you know. Have you ever noticed that when someone hates you, sometimes you do things to make them hate you even more?

"I'm sure it'll be clear by the wedding," I add, biting into my sandwich.

Too late. Damage is done!

4

ICE CREAM AND WINE

Ash laughs at my outburst. I hardly think it's very funny. He's leaning back on the couch, as he always does when he's into a basketball game on TV. Now he's laughing at my misery. I'm so unhappy, I feel my stupid wigglies moving all over my head. Shit, Asher probably sees them too, but he doesn't care. He's used to my stupid hair.

"Is that why you were so quiet in the car?" he asks.

Uh, yeah.

I sip my red wine. It's smooth and perfect. It's the same red blend Hades kept drinking and complaining about. I really wanted something in the restaurant, but I'd learned to never drink around Sandra. Never. I mean, if I had done that, I might be apologizing to Ash for sucking out one of her eyeballs, you know.

"She thinks I don't drink," I say, drinking more. Standing over the sofa, I offer the glass to him. He shakes his head. "She thinks I'm not cool—just a total loser working in a library. Well, Asher, I should tell you that more people should try *just working in a library*. It's quiet and I happen to absolutely love it. But it's obviously not as cool as the hoity-toity stuff she's working on... What the hell is she doing again after graduation?"

"Paralegal," he says with a nod, his eyes glued to the screen. He hits his knee over a missed basket.

"Right. Paralegal. I mean—" I gulp down more red wine. "Next year she's going to be sticking her uppity nose right into all sorts of books, like me, isn't she? So what's better? Huh? Doing that in the office or beside a tranquil waterfall in a beautiful university library? I'll enjoy trips to Tahiti and the moon in the arms of a nice strong man in my romance novels any day over contract disputes and a bunch of legal shit. She treats me as if I'm an absolute zero, Ash. Like I'm not worth her time."

"I don't think she gets you," Ash says, "that's all. You know... you walk around in those old clothes and thick glasses. She treats you like Gorgiana, not Medusa. She thinks you're delicate. Then she's totally shocked when you act like Medusa."

"Yeah," I say with a nod and another sip. "My hair wanted to circle 'round her neck and strangle her."

I drink more wine over that, nearly finishing the glass. Then I fall silent. There's just the noise of the basketball game from the TV. Ash turns back to the game. Maybe he doesn't like picturing his sister being choked to death by a bunch of my snakes. Or maybe he's just that into the game.

I walk over to the fridge and grab a carton of ice cream and a large metal spoon. I need that now. Ice cream and wine. It's the absolute best combination, I tell you, when you're pissed off about something. I always recommend that people try it whenever they've had a rotten day. Ice cream and wine. Except, we only have chocolate in the fridge. I mean, I love chocolate ice cream, but vanilla goes so much better with red wine.

"She's prying into how my parents have the money for the place," I continue from the kitchen. "It's a great venue. It's gonna be totally Tuscany, Ash, and reminds me of Portofino, you know. I mean, I'd want to get married there. But I don't like lying to her about how my parents, who, you know, have been dead for like three thousand years, are picking up the bill."

"She's going to love you for paying for it, Gorge," he hollers from the other room.

"She's not acting like it." I lean my hands on the kitchen counter staring at a Lucky Charms cereal box. Lucky Charms helps bad moods too. It's so great with those tiny, sweet marshmallows. I fucking love Lucky Charms. Maybe I should get some of that too?

"You're so worked up, Gorgi."

"She's just a meany."

"She's Sandra."

"Doesn't she drive you crazy?"

"Yes, Gorge. She's Sandra."

"Well, how can you be so nice about it?"

Because he's Asher.

"How'd you do on your syntax final, babe?" I ask, trying to change the subject. Then I thrust a huge spoon in the freshly opened ice cream carton. I love looking at the lovely chocolate goo as I scoop a big chunk. Then I throw a huge spoonful in my mouth. "That boring grammar class, talking about words and signs," I say with my mouth full. "Did I mess up your grades?"

"I got an A."

"Should have guessed it," I say with my mouth still full. "Good job. You're so smart. I'm so glad our terrible fight didn't mess everything up."

I walk over, carrying the carton of ice cream and my glass of wine. I lay it all on the coffee table. Then I sit down beside him on the couch with the ice cream carton on my lap. I scoop another huge spoonful and offer it to him. He shakes his head. So I shrug and throw a whole other giant spoonful in my mouth.

"It's good," I say with my mouth full. "Sure you don't want some? It's chocolate. Your favorite."

He shakes his head. Then he laughs and runs his hand along my arm.

I jump up and walk over to my fireplace. I peruse my relics. I call these odds and ends collected over the centuries my relics. They're priceless. When I first met Ash, bitch-Athena came to my house and lit all my relics on fire. But these were hidden in my closet. I've lost many relics over the years. When you live for thousands of years, it's so hard to keep anything, you know. That is part of what makes the ones I still have so valuable.

I pick up a small black statue of Hercules. And next to that is a drawing of Lucrezia de Lucan. They're both pieces of art by Antonio Pollaiuolo. He was an artist in Italy during the Renaissance. Yeah, I knew Anthony. But I didn't get up to admire his work. I wanted to look at good ole Lucrezia de Lucan. She's this girl with curly hair and a faint smile. Antonio never painted this drawing. And the girl, in real life, never gave much more than that faint smile she's got in the sketch. She was a complete meany too and reminds me of Ash's sister. But Lucrezia's brother, Lorenzo, well, I adored him like I adore Asher.

Speaking of the love of my life, Asher jumps up and looks over my shoulder at my art.

"I always liked this statue," Ash says. He's not looking at Lady Lucan; he's studying the athletic bronze. "What is this depicting, Gorgi?"

"Hercules."

Ash holds the statue in his palm, tracing the man's

ripped musculature with his thumb. I always liked the muscles on the statue too. I glance at Ash's yummy chest. That makes me hungry. So I put the sketch of the bitch down and pick up my ice cream and spoon again.

"It's by Antonio Pollaiuolo," I say, dipping into more luscious chocolate goo. "It's a model statue for a much larger one of Hercules. I knew Anthony, you know, Ash. But before you ask, I didn't know Hercules."

Ash laughs.

That artist Antonio Pollaiuolo totally had a crush on me. You can see why I'm loaded. But I don't keep all this stuff for money. I keep these priceless things to remind me of my past. And Lorenzo.

Sigh. Lorenzo was such a sweet guy.

Like Asher. Right. And now Ash's white T-shirt is reflecting green, and I'm reflecting on how his abs are not much different from those on the rippled Hercules figurine. He notices and I turn away and, instead of ripping his shirt like you want me to do, Medusa, I stuff more ice cream into my mouth.

But he is beside me, holding me. He's about to lean down and kiss my lips, but he brushes hair from my eyes instead. It's probably a stupid wiggly. Why does this guy like me? That upsets me enough to rush back to the couch and fall into it, folding my arms in a total huff.

"You're so worked up tonight," Ash says with a laugh.

"I'm worried. How am I going to pull off your sister's wedding? I can't be in pictures. Especially now that she wants to do it in broad daylight. She can't even guess the horror she'd feel, reviewing her photos later."

"She doesn't know there are snakes in her family now," he quips with a smirk. Then he laughs. He thinks that's *so funny.* I don't.

I lean against his shoulder. I run a stray hand over his perfect blond surfer hair.

"It's going to be okay, Gorgi."

"There you go saying that again. I wish I could believe it. I'm going to be meeting your parents too."

"Is that what this is about? You can't act like you didn't know you'd fight with my sister."

"I know."

"My mom and dad are going to love you."

"What makes you think that?"

"My parents, unlike my sister, aren't critical—especially when it comes to things I like. I think they're going to like you a lot."

"God, I hope so, Ash," I say, snuggling into his shoulder again—but not before I lick more ice cream. I sigh. "I don't know, it's not just meeting your family, it's the pictures. I can't get pictures taken."

Ash turns to face me, but he avoids my eyes.

"You don't get it, Gorge. If you don't want pictures taken, go and hide. Sandra and Jack won't care. You already won them over by paying for the wedding. Actually ... my mom might care."

"She'll want the pictures perfect."

"No, she'll want pictures of my new girlfriend." Then he kisses my lips. I *love* that.

He's so cute, Gorgi.

"Really?" I ask, snuggling closer to my man's hard chest. He's got this nice woodsy cologne I love. "You're so sweet, Ash."

We smooch more.

But then my cellphone rings between kisses. It's in my baggy pants pocket. I ignore it, smooching more. But it buzzes again.

The contact says *Cora.*

"Hey, Cora. What's up?"

"Hi, Gorgi. How you guys holding up?"

"As good as can be. We can talk now?"

"Yes."

"Are Moros and Gabriel safe?"

"Moros is becoming an absolute brat. She's like a teenager in a little tyke's body. Grace is always taking her to town, and you know Gracie is not the best influence. God knows what the hell she's letting my girl see. But who the fuck am I to care? And Moros loves Grace and Gabe so much. Gabriel's wonderful, as always. Hashan is Hashan. And Grace, you know—"

"Who cares 'bout Grace?"

Cora laughs. "I know, Gorge. It's funny because she's always asking about you."

"I don't care."

"Hey, Cora," Ash says over my shoulder into the phone.

"Tall, blond, and handsome's with you?"

"Yeah. So what's up, Cora?"

"Well, things are good enough for us to talk, but not good enough for me to head down. I'm afraid the heat's going up again. Sunland is not secure. You're right to ask about my family. We're all in danger. It's too unsafe for me to visit, though I'd give anything to see you and watch over you guys right now. Especially after Hades told me what happened."

"Just protect your family."

"I know. Did Hades tell you about the jar?"

"Yeah. You never told me about it. I thought Pandora's Jar was just a legend. And I never heard anything about Mandrigels."

"That's not true, Gorge. I told you lots about Engel. I told you all about my mother and, anytime I speak of Nephree, you know I mention Engel. Nephree and Engel were the closest of friends. But I thought he was lost long ago, just like the jar."

"What can I do, Cora?"

"Well, this is going to really suck, but I think you and Asher should lay low again. I don't want you going out in public. They're watching. Hades has agents of his own all over your neighborhood, but Imada is everywhere."

"I can't this time, Cora."

"Why?"

"There's a wedding."

"Are you two getting married? Are you fucking kidding me, Gorgiana! I'm so happy for you!"

Asher laughs. He can obviously hear us. He's got the volume of the TV on low.

"No, Cora." I laugh and look at Ash, running a hand along his arm. "Mr. Perfect hasn't proposed yet." Asher nods slowly, raising his eyebrow. Then I add teasingly, "*Yet*. I'm arranging a wedding for his sister. It's happening in two weeks."

"Oh. That's not good timing."

A moment later, she says, "Well, the event is still a few weeks away. Just stay indoors for the next two weeks so we can clear out the rest of the riff raff. We can guard you guys if you stay at your house. Don't go to work. Keep Asher home from lectures. He can take some sick days. And message Aner if Engel shows up. We know he's looking for you. And then, God, if you do see Engel, give him my regards. I so hope to meet him again."

"Okay."

"Unless...you've seen him?"

"Hades asked that too. No, Cora, I haven't seen him."

"Arachne told him he could trust you. Engel will show up. But his secrecy is infectious. He knows how to hide. And he won't cooperate with us."

"Why, Cora?"

There's silence on the phone for a moment. I look over at the game. Ash slaps his leg again. His team isn't doing so hot.

"Gorgi," Cora finally says, more quietly, "the Mandrigel dwarfs were Hades's slaves. Remember when I told you I froze the fires in Tartarus? It stopped the machines that were running our city. The Mandrigel were no longer needed to stoke the fires. But before that, Hades enslaved them. But not only that…he tortured them, Gorge. He did terrible things to Engel's people. Nephrea fought Hades and freed them. So Engel talks to me, out of respect for Nephree, but barely. And he won't ever trust me. Even though I helped free his people, I was still queen when his people suffered. And Hades…never."

"Never mind Engel, Cora. What about Arachne? I heard they questioned her? Is she okay?"

"She's fine, Gorgi. She was captured before you saw her ice the bay. Before she gave you the scepter. She's as safe as when you left Portofino."

"Thank god."

"Yeah. Okay, Gorge. Text *Aner* if there's an emergency. And say bye to that cute boy of yours. When the danger clears, you guys should come up to Toronto again. Maybe we can have your wedding up here?"

"We're not getting married," shouts Asher.

Cora laughs. "Bye, Gorge."

"Bye, Cora."

I stuff the phone back in my pants pocket.

Then I reach to the table for my ice cream. I scoop some more delicious brown goo into my mouth. The carton's half empty now. I'm really pigging out. You know I can, though. It's yet another benefit of being an immortal ugly viper. I can magically eat a ton of food without a bellyache. So I have more. Because Cora's call, though I love her to death, actually made me feel worse. I was so busy thinking of the wedding that I forgot about my real problem at hand: Imada.

Ash turns off the TV. Then he squeezes my hand.

"Why'd you shut the game off?"

"God, Gorgi, I can feel how nervous you are. Everything's gonna be all right."

"You keep saying that," I say with a long sigh. "But, you know, as bad as your sister was, she got my mind off Imada." I heave another sigh. Even yummy ice cream isn't enough now. I put my head in my hands, running my hands through my hair.

"Everything will be fine, Gorge," Ash says, rubbing my back. "I'll call in sick with my professors."

"How come you keep saying we'll be fine?"

"Because we're together," he says with a big grin. Then he leans over and pecks me on the cheek. I kiss his lips.

"That is soooo corny, Ash. I mean, couldn't you think of something better to say?"

"It's true."

We kiss some more over that.

"Umm," I say, "this beats ice cream."

As we smooch, our tongues run along each other and we hold each other more tightly. He pulls my body closer and even touches my long hair—*I like that.* I know you do, Medusa. God, I love him. But that's the problem. Being with him keeps putting him in danger.

We had a fight a few months ago over that. Remember? I told him I didn't love him and I never wanted to see him again. I didn't let him into my house. I got all crazy because I wanted us to be over. I stopped everything. And then...

He came over the next day.

Yep. He's a total nutjob. You know, Asher is crazier than I am. And now, he proves it by reaching under my granny sweater and blouse, sneaking a hand under my bra, and rubbing his fingers over my breasts and my nipples.

"I heard Cora say the heat's going up," Ash says between kisses, pulling up my sweater and shirt. My unclasped bra falls between my legs.

"That's corny too, Ash." We laugh.

I help remove his T-shirt. And yes, sure, wouldn't you know it, but looking at his ripped abs and chest makes me only feel hotter—it's not much different than that bronze figurine.

He's so hot.

I surprise him by throwing him back on the sofa and moving on top of him, straddling him between my legs. He pulls me close. Then he wraps his arms around me. And I'm grinding on him.

"You know when I get worried," I say, "I also get excited."

"Everything's going to be fine," he quips.

He pulls down my baggy pants. So I undo his belt and unzip his pants. Then I yank them down.

It's still raining outside. I can see the yard in my green mind's eye. Or, rather, I can smell it. I smell my small backyard with the tall trees under the clouds. I have a single table and chair out there getting soaked. I left a book I'm borrowing on the table. Well, it's drenched now. I'll have to think up something to tell Charlie, my boss, over that one. Anyway, the arousal, and my worry, has heightened my senses. In the front yard—

His fingers are reaching inside my panties. He's touching me down there.

Fuck, that feels good!

In the front yard is a lovely gray wood veranda, with columns, that looks out on the street. And I have another table with two chairs on the deck. Usually, there are tons of students riding by, even at this time, on the street. Not now. It must be the rain. There are no cars driving by on—

Fuck!

He enters with a finger. Now his finger is coming in and out of my pussy. Then another two fingers. I lean down, kissing his lips hard again. Then my fingers run through his wavy hair.

I'm looking down at his ripped chest. It's glowing green from my eyes. A stray snake runs along his neck then rides along his pecs. I slap it. I hate them! I fucking hate my hair! Then I wonder: oh God, did he just see my head full of all those fucking vipers?

I lean over him on the couch and just hold him tight. He runs kisses along my neck.

I grab some ice cream and a spoon—but after I take a last swig of wine, finishing the glass.

"What are you doing?" he asks.

"Well, there's really nothing better than ice cream and wine when having sex. Care for some?"

He laughs and shakes his head. Then he scoots forward and removes his underwear. It falls to his feet, and I help him kick it off. Then I hold his cock in one hand and put the ice cream down with my other.

I straddle his lap and touch my lips to his. Then I feel him inch his way inside me. And now I'm moving up and down on him, slowly, as he's fucking me.

"Yes, Ash. Yes. Fuck me."

The entire city of Sunland shows up green inside my head. Despite the rain, I can smell the university, and envision the lamps along the walkways, a couple miles away. There are a few students walking about now, mostly with umbrellas. Then I locate my job. My library. It's an old building. Decades old. I loved that when I first took the job. My awareness opens up even further to the inside of the building. It's closed, but a few dim lights are on in the offices, behind their windowed walls. The fountain's on and a few stray lights dimly light the main hall, lined with bookshelves. But the library is abandoned. Next my senses zero in on the swamps surrounding Sunland. On one side is the beach. On the other are miles upon miles of marshland. Humans think it's quiet at night—not with my nose. I see frogs and snakes under the thrush. Scores of alligators are lying about among the nearby bogs. I love them. I even spot our mascot, Allie the Alligator, who's just floating in utter darkness along the water on our campus.

Then I jump. Someone is running not far from where Ash and I hid last week. He's in a suit. He lowers his head to his shoulder, I think to contact someone by walkie talkie. Then, zeroing in, I notice even under green light that he smells as if he's wearing black. Cora wasn't kidding. Agents are all over the place. I can't tell which are friendly and which aren't.

I spot three more moving from the bushes. They're close to the edge of campus, near the university store. They seem to be on the perimeter of campus. Still, they're a few miles from my house.

My tits are being squeezed. And I hear my man breathing heavily. I grab one of his fingers, take it up to my lips, and kiss it. But I don't suck on his fingers. I can't. I'm so excited that my fangs are pressing against my lips. And, shit, that means my hair—*but it feels so fucking good.* Up and down. I'm moving faster and breathing more heavily.

"I love you, Asher."

The whole room has changed from yellow to green. And as I turn, a green beacon moves along my walls.

"Let me kiss your lips," he says.

"I can't, Ash. I can't."

"Your teeth?"

I nod. "Just make love to me. Yes. Fuck me... Oh, shit, I'm coming. I'm coming!"

I fall, spent, on my man.

But he's not done. He's still grinding inside me. *But...* he's not the only one moving. Although my mind is rushing through all the images in the miles surrounding my home, I smell a very faint rustle of leaves right beside my house. Right here. I see eyes. Even through the green filter through which I receive images via my nose, I couldn't mistake the color. They smell as bright blue as Cora's. They look like hers. Or that vile man, Hades. They are a shiny azure blue. And, oddly, his face is tinged the same color. Those eyes are now staring at me, between the drapes, through a side window. He is staring with a gaping mouth. At first, I don't understand why he looks surprised. Then it dawns on me that he sees us naked. No, that's not it, either. I'm not only naked; I'm having sex with a man on my couch. But, no, that's not it either. Not only am I naked and having sex, my thick vipers are hissing wildly over my head.

"Oh, Gorgi," Ash says, sinking down under me.

I turn my head to look at the intruder at our living room window. He looks away and makes a run for it.

I leap up from the couch like a cat. Ash doesn't have time to respond. I run at full speed straight through my side window. It leads directly to the backyard; the front door would take too long. But...

Fuck, that hurt!

There wasn't only glass there, you know, there was wood siding. Why am I always running through windows?!

"Gorgi!" cries Ash from behind me. "You're not dressed!"

Like I care right now. I feel violated by that little shit. Whatever this thing is—this Mandrigel?—Engel?—he had no business watching us. But I can't think straight. For a moment, I long to be in Ash's embrace again. We were just together making love, weren't we?

The rain's pouring. That makes it harder to smell. But I'm tuned in enough to see all the black-suited agents rushing to my house. Did they see the Mandrigel too?

"Medusa," says someone about five yards from me. He cocks a gun and points it at my head. A snake snatches his hand in the dark before he can say another stupid word. The snake tugs him closer and I grab his arm. Then I snap his wrist.

He screams.

I turn the man's head toward mine. He's wearing shades. It's a fucking Imada agent, for sure.

I yank off the shades and stare right into his eyes, illuminating his face with green light. His body falls limp into my arms. He's petrified.

But he's not dead.

Or is he? I look down. He's lying on the ground, and I've dismembered him. His hand is severed from his arm now.

FUCKING KILL HIM!

But he's not after Ash or me; he's after that little blue man and...

Ash is in danger!

Where did Engel go? Hades wasn't kidding, he's wily, all right. I can't smell him. That's impossible. He couldn't have gone far enough to evade my sense of smell. Where did he go?

But it's only pouring harder.

The agent wakes up. I quickly take his head in both hands and snap his neck. He falls limp onto the ground.

Was that completely necessary, Medusa?

Yep.

I lift my head and take a big whiff. Water is pouring down my face. About twenty agents are leaving the university grounds, converging toward my house with guns raised. But they're still a mile away.

"Engel?" I ask. I'm surprised by the pleasantness of my voice. No matter how vile a monster I change into, I always have that same dainty voice. I've always hated my soft voice. "Engel. Come out. I saw you watching us."

But why would he show himself? The snakes are slithering all over my head, my eyes are glowing emerald, and I feel my sharp fangs biting at my bottom lip. I'm a full-on freak monster show.

I shine my green eyes all over my side yard. Nothing. All I hear is the rain. I don't smell him either...no, someone else is approaching. I hear leaves crack. I turn.

Asher covers his eyes.

"What's going on!" he asks. He's drenched, wearing only sweatpants in the pouring rain.

"I saw him."

"Who?"

"Engel."

Asher comes closer, but then he quickly steps back. He must see the body lying on the ground.

"Go back inside, Ash. It's not safe out here."

He heads back, but as he's nearly inside, I holler, "Wait, text *Aner*. Tell him we need help *now*."

After Asher goes back in the house through the hole in the wall I just made, my head whips my drenched snake-hair left and right. I'm sniffing down the wet street. Thank god it's raining so hard. Sure, it might be too wet to smell much, but no one on the street can see me lurking about with snakes in my hair either.

A police car quietly drives down the road toward my house. It's weirdly driving without its headlights on.

I look down at the dead body. I see water dripping down

my breasts. That's when I remember that I'm still completely naked.

A man gets out of the car. It's a bald man in a black suit. This isn't Imada, it's "Aner." Or Hades.

"Where did Engel go?" Hades hollers.

I crouch as much as I can behind my wall to hide my nakedness. "I don't know. I saw him, but he's gone."

"All right, Medusa. Go back inside. Stay inside until it's safe."

"There's a man dead here. An agent. I had to protect Ash."

"I'll take care of it."

5

———

JUST A TASTE

I know Cora told me to stay home, but tonight's the night of Sandra's wedding tasting. Asher would have come too if it wasn't for an important meeting with a professor. And it's been over a week. So, I mean, as much as I'm a homebody, I mean, *come on. A week?* Staying in my house that long gets a bit nutty, even for me. Well, the problem, of course, is that our lovely, picturesque Italy in Orlando venue is outdoors and it's pouring rain. My nasty quip about it possibly raining is becoming a very real possibility. Not only does that make the upcoming event nail-biting; it means that the wedding tasting can't be done at the venue location. I suggested we try my favorite place again, The Cookie Cutter, to try out the food. Sandra said fine, but she didn't sound very happy about it.

I think it's raining worse than last time. As I shake all the drops from my umbrella and coat, the maître d' directs me to another of those huge booths I love. Sandra picked a place just like before, not far from the windows and outdoor patio.

I'm nervous. I don't care about pictures and the wedding right now. I'm worried about the risk I'm taking being outside my home. I'm checking every corner of the restaurant for any sign of danger. My eyes and ears—and nose— are hyperaware.

I scoot across from Sandra in the booth. She's sipping a clear martini again, this time dressed up in black—a black sweater, skirt, and bowery hat. She's always dressed fashionably, but wearing all black is dark for her. She usually likes color. This kinda looks mod. And her dark eyeliner, which is usually lovely on her face, looks almost goth. No...wait...the makeup is running down her face. What the hell?

"They're bringing pizza," she says, throwing her fingers frivolously up in the air. "Pizza. Okay? Pizza." Then she gulps down half her drink and seems to have a hard time swallowing.

She looks at me. Squints. Then she says, "Well, you look good—" She covers her mouth to hold back a burp. "In that same old sweater." Then the bitch bursts out in inappropriate laughter. I'm wearing my usual granny sweater, pants, and goggle glasses. I ignore her insult. I mean, it feels harsher than ever, but she's obviously in some weird mood.

"What's the matter, Sandra?" I take off my goggle glasses. "What the hell happened?"

"What do you think? Hmm? What else fuckin' goes wrong in my life?" Then she looks deep into my eyes. She shakes her head. "You have such beautiful golden eyes. Why do you block them with those dumb thick glasses?"

"Let's not talk about me," I say, shaking out my long hair. I think some raindrops hit her again. She doesn't seem to care. I turn away. "This is for you."

"It's off." She downs the rest of her drink. "The whole fuckin' thing's off. That's all."

Oh.

"He's a fun guy, Jack, you know. We were always off somewhere. Just a week ago he commented on all this rain."

She folds her arms and glares out the window. "I hate Florida. I really hate living here. Anyway, he said we should get some sun. So we flew to Jamaica."

"That sounds nice."

"Right? Well, that was the start of the end of everything. We always fight, but, boy, did we fight then. Jack doesn't have a lot of money, even though he acts like he does. The whole trip was a complete disaster: the small rinky-dink plane, dirty buses, walking the streets in the dead of night; in the rain, Gorgi, in the rain. I mean I could have died out there. When we got back, I think that had already made things sour. The thing about him is—"

"Hey," she says to a waitress walking by. "Get me another one of these, will ya?" And she laughs inappropriately again.

"I'll tell your waiter," the waitress says.

Sandra closes her eyes tightly for a moment. Then she smiles with that fake grin she loves to show me. She looks toward the window and raises her empty cocktail glass to her lips with a shaky hand.

"The thing about him is—" I remind her, gesticulating for her to continue.

"He dreams up shit. He gets ideas no man can fulfill. That made me fall for him. But he can never match them. Thing is... I mean who cares about the fact that the plane almost crashed, right? I could have thrown up bouncing up and down like that. The turbulence, or the pilot, was awful. Then we didn't even have a hotel room. That was maddening enough. Walking dark downtown streets in the middle of the night in torrential rain was horrible. And dangerous."

"So that's why the wedding's off?"

"No." Then she bursts into laughter more than ever. "That's not it. He's a liar. A cheat. He told me he was in law school." She shakes her head. "Not even close." She sips from her empty glass again. Then she stares at it and hammers her fist on the table. "Where's another drink! Fuck!" She runs her hands through her long hair. "The most he's not goin' to get is not getting professional gambling. I mean...he went to college—*I think*. But his money, the little he's got, comes from Mommy and Daddy. He's always busy either playing with the Xbox or with himself. He's a total dickhead. What do you think, Gorgi? About that?"

"I don't believe it."

"Yeah." She raises her empty glass. It shakes in her hand again, and I'm wondering how many she's drunk.

She slowly nods.

The waitress brings over another martini.

"I say, fuck him. Fuck him. Okay?" She closes her eyes for a moment. Then she slams her palm on the table. The waitress turns from another line of booths. "I mean *fuuuckk him! Fuck him! I tell you. Fuck him, Gorgi!*"

I look around. A few people have turned to look at us. Then Sandra bursts into laughter.

"So you left him?"

"*No!*" she shouts at me. "I di-dd-na fuckin' leave him, stupid. That's not it. That's not it at all... Well, it sort of is. But that's not why. I was just coming to grips with marrying a loser. I was trying to work shit out, all the shit after Jamaica. I was going to go on and still marry the jerk."

Another waitress comes with a bunch of platters of sliced pizza. There are all kinds of toppings: sausage, pepperoni, ham, mixed vegetables, cheese, etc., etc. It looks delicious. With a waiter's help, she places all the dishes on our table.

"Bon appetite," the waiter and waitress say with a big grin.

Sandra moans, rubbing her forehead.

Then she drinks her fresh martini.

"Go ahead," she says to me, gesturing to the platter. "You might as well enjoy it. Maybe we can arrange the same thing when you marry my brother."

"Ash and I are not planning on getting married."

She just raises her eyebrows at me.

I grab a few small slices. It looks absolutely delicious. They're very fancy-schmancy, cut in bite-size quarters. And she actually listened to me about having a thin crust. But then, before I stuff one in my mouth, I look over at her. She has her head in her hand, holding back tears. It's so depressing, I lose my appetite.

"It was three days ago." She turns to the window to her left. Tears run down her cheeks. "You know, his apartment is not far from you and Ash. Well, I was returning from the library. Jack told me he couldn't make it that night so—"

All of a sudden, I smell something hellish. I mean, actual hellfire stuff. At first it mixes with Sandra's perfume, and it's hard for me to discern. Then an acrid smell fills my nostrils: bitter with stinky sulfur. It's faint, but distinctive. That's the smell of bullets and guns. Why? Why here? Where is it coming from? Normally, I wouldn't notice, but my snakes are hyperalert. I chose to risk not tying them into a bun tonight. And with the rain washing away any outdoor scent, the indoor smell is quite recognizable.

This stench is emanating from three black-suited men walking from a black SUV. The black suits are wearing shades. I smell them in my green mind's eye. They're under the awning and approaching an open door to the restaurant. I have an urge to jump up and run, but Sandra chose the absolute worst time ever to tell me her disaster story, and it's all she can do to not burst into tears. I've never even seen Sandra cry. Then it's all I can do to not have my hair move to my right, toward the front of the restaurant. Them wigglies are ready to lengthen.

Imada, Gorgi. Imada!

I know. I know.

I press down hard on my hair to keep them wigglies in line. I should have tied them.

"Thought I'd just spend the night alone," Sandra's continuing. "That was okay. I didn't care. So I brought home some pizza. Pizza. I love pizza. How goddamn ironic, right?" She laughs again but there's nothing funny. "I hear someone in our bedroom. I think it's a total intruder. So I rush over. And there it is. The two of them. My good friend from my political science class, Amelia, is naked with her tits being slammed down on white sheets under the naked ass of my asshole fiancé. They're screwing each other *in OUR FUCKING BEDROOM!*"

Shut her up!

She screams. More people turn from nearby tables.

"*I mean, FUCK!*"

SHUT HER UP NOW, GORGI!

Sandra starts to sob with her head in her hands. "I mean *FUCK!*" she says again, hammering the table with her fists.

The three black suits are inside. But they've stopped. I barely hear something, with my monster ears, about them going in different directions. I smell one of them cock a pistol under his trench coat. My ears, though hypersensitive, can't hear their conversation. Maybe it's the rain outdoors, it must be the rain. Water is splashing hard against the windows. And Sandra is bawling.

All of a sudden, Sandra grabs a bunch of slices of pizza and stuffs as many as she can in her mouth.

"I mean, fuck it," she says with her mouth full. "Right! Fuck it. *What a fucking dick!*"

"Did you drive here?" I ask.

"Hmm?... What?" She wipes her eyes and squints at me like I'm a complete nutjob. And even now, in her misery, she's got that all-too-familiar pompous well-I'm-better-than-you-anyway look on her face. "Huh?"

I jump up. She mutters something else between more pizza dough and cheese in her mouth as I drag her away from the booth. There's a glass door leading outside onto a small, drenched patio. I throw the glass door open.

We're met with the sound of torrential rain. Now that's bad because it makes my image of our pursuers less clear.

"Hey! What are you doing! Hey, Gorgi...what's happening to your hair?"

Yep, it's thickening. But she's so surprised by our sudden escape, and so inebriated, that she thinks it's funny. Now she's laugh-crying.

No time to talk. I'm dragging her through the drenched parking lot.

"Hey, what's going on!" she finally says, yanking her arm away from me.

Her eyes bulge. Because she sees my face. And judging by the green light shining over her face, my skin is probably wrinkled like an old lady's and I've probably grown fangs. And I know them wigglies on my head are slithering.

"What the hell is—"

I'm carrying her. There's no time to explain.

She knows now.

Like I care.

Protect her.

I know, Medusa. I know.

"Where's your car, Sandra? You drove like last time, right?"

"What the fuck is going on, Gorgi! Your hair! Eww! Eww! Is that? It looks like...are those...oh my God... are those snakes? *I hate snakes!*"

"Your car, Sandra!" I repeat. I stare right into her eyes. That shuts her up. Between her terror of my transformation, my emerald eyes, and her shock, she's too overwhelmed to object. Not to mention the magic, mesmerizing power of my eyes. She points a shaky finger to a blue BMW. Her whole hand is flapping. I rush through the pouring rain still carrying her under my arm.

Back in the restaurant, I catch a whiff of an agent searching our booth. The other two agents stayed back by the front door. But it's gone as quickly as it came. The rain is dulling my senses.

"We have to go." I look deep into her eyes again with my glowing green ones. It calms her. A little. And as weird as I look, I still have the same Gorgiana voice. "We have to leave. Do you understand? Your life is in danger."

She nods over and over, staring transfixed into my green eyes. I turn because even a woman will freeze if she looks long enough. Then I grab her purse. I find her keys and open the door of her car.

Then I stop. What the hell am I doing! I can't drive. But I can't let her drive either. She's drunk. I don't know how to drive. Who's going to drive us?

"What's the matter?" she asks beside me. "Gor... Gor... Gorgi?"

"I don't know how to drive."

Sandra bursts out in laughter. It's so weird that it makes me stop moving.

"Have you looked in the mirror?" Sandra blurts out. "Of course a fearsome beast doesn't know how to fucking drive! Are you kidding me! What the fuck else can go wrong tonight. Why do you look—"

"Hey!" she exclaims.

I pull her toward the other side of the car. Then I throw open the passenger's door and push her in. Then I run to the driver's side. I sit down and look, bewildered, at the dashboard.

"Press on the brake pedal," she says. She looks out the window. "God, it's raining so hard. Look at all the small drops of water." And she traces one on the passenger's window.

Look, I know where the brake pedal is, okay? It's just been about thirty years since I pressed it. That was to stop a car from falling off a cliff. Anyway, she presses a button for me and the car starts. Then I press on the gas, and we're thrown forward about two inches, nearly hitting the car in front of us.

"Hey! Reverse first!"

I press the middle pedal. Then I reverse, staring at the picture of the lot behind us on the dashboard. Sandra moves the middle doohickie to the "D" position. Then she reaches over and turns on the windshield wipers.

We rocket back into our seats as I hit the gas.

Now we're just turning, so everything will be fine. Right?

Just get her out of here!

I know. I know.

We turn onto a street. I swerve a little too much and feel the car lose its grip, hearing the wheels squeal. But then we shimmy back onto the road. That's when I see a dark SUV driving fast right behind us.

"Eww!" Sandra says. "Yuck! One of your hairs touched me! Is it hair? No. It's...it's slimy and it *has eyes!* Snakes? *I hate snakes!* I fucking hate snakes! Oh, god, what else could go wrong tonight? I fucking hate snakes!"

And I hate you.

The SUV is coming close on our tail.

"That was a red light, Gorgiana," Sandra says, pointing behind us. "You were supposed to stop. You have to stop at all the red lights."

I turn suddenly, way too hard, and we drift into the next street, nearly riding over the curb onto the sidewalk.

"I should have let them just capture me," says a stranger, a male voice, behind me. I look in the rearview mirror. There's a small man with a blue face in the back seat.

"*Oh my God!*" cries Sandra. "*Oh my God! What's that? What the hell is that?! What the hell!*"

Sandra's screaming hysterically. She can't stop screaming.

"Calm down, Sandra!" I shout.

I look in the mirror again at the short man with the blue face. And those bright blue eyes, just like Cora's. He's old with wrinkled skin. He's wearing clothes that are in tatters. It's a plain beige shirt and baggy pants the likes of which I haven't seen since the 1920s.

"*What is that!*" cries Sandra. "*What the hell is in my car!*"

"Engel?" I ask.

"Ciao, Medusa," Engel says behind me with a nod. I recognize an Italian accent. Of course he'd have that. He lived in Portofino, Italy, for the past century. And he sounds quite cheery, despite all the chaos. "I've found my Guardian."

"*Is this some kind of fucking circus!*" Sandra shouts at me. "*Like you dress up, Gorgi, with snakes in your hair and then we get acrobats and small circus freaks—*"

"I'm not from a circus, signora," objects Engel.

"What the hell are you!" Sandra cries. "Eww!" She's hysterical. "Another snake brushed against my arm. Another snake! Keep them the fuck off me, Gorgi! God, what is going on here! God! I mean, *what the fuck is going on!* Why is there an elf behind us!"

"I'm not an elf."

"I'll explain it all when I get you home, Sandra."

You can't take her home, Gorgi. They'll just shoot her the minute she steps out of the car.

"Stop the car," rages Sandra. "Okay. Stop my fucking car

right now. You're gonna wreck it. I spent everything on this car. We're going to hit a wall. You can't drive, that's for fucking sure. I see it now. So stop my fucking car!"

"Engel, do they know you're in here?"

"No, Guardian." He looks behind him at the pursuing black SUV. "I followed you two inside."

"Are you *certain* they never saw you get into the car?"

"Sì, they don't know I'm here, Guardian," he says. "I'm sure of it."

"Call me Gorgi," I say to Engel. "Maybe they're just chasing me."

"Why the fuck would anyone be chasing *you*, Gorgi?" Sandra asks. And I think I even hear a chuckle.

They don't know Engel's in the car. Do you know what that means? It's only three of them chasing us. If you get rid of them, this will all be over. You can let me take care of them.

Yeah.

Stop the fucking car. Let me take care of them.

Not here in public.

More will come if you don't fight now!

I run two more red lights, nearly hitting a truck's fender. Sandra, of course, is screaming again. I don't stop. Then I recognize this area. We're close to the beach. I know the beach like the back of my hand, because I walk here all the time, alone, in the middle of the night. I see the roads leading to beach homes. Sandra cries out again as I hit another car turning down one of the narrow streets. Then she screams some more as I press the accelerator pedal to the floor, speeding toward a fence at the end of a narrow road. Engel's so quiet that I wonder if he's still in the car.

I know beyond the fence is just sand. And I know the beach will be empty in the pouring rain.

The car hurdles over a curb and through a wooden

fence. Then we're bumping up and down like crazy on the sand.

"That's it!" cries Sandra. "I've had enough! Oh my god! Gorgi, stop the car! Now!" She flaps a finger toward the ocean. "Oh, my god! Stop the car! Do you want us to drive into the ocean?"

Our pursuers are right behind us.

Sorry about this, Sandra.

I slam on the brakes. Their SUV plows into the back of Sandra's car. And Sandra's right, we stop right near an incoming wave.

"You okay?" I ask, turning to Sandra.

Sandra doesn't turn. She doesn't even move. She's staring out the windshield.

"Stay in the car." I accidentally let out a growl and Sandra jumps, lurching back in terror against the passenger's door. She tries to open the door with a shaky hand, but I reach over her and make sure it's locked. "You and Engel stay put in the car. Okay? Keep your heads down. Don't get up and don't leave no matter what. They'll shoot you."

Sandra nods, shaking.

I throw open my door.

I sniff. I smell only a couple bystanders by the road, about a hundred yards away, on the street we just jettisoned from. It's hard to be sure, though, as water pours over me. A girl is standing at a stoplight with a dog under an umbrella. A man is rushing along the street with a bag over his head to shield him from the rain. The beach itself is completely empty.

The back window of Sandra's BMW shatters. It's a gunshot.

We can't let them hurt them, Medusa.

Oh, don't you worry. Bring them to me.

But we shouldn't kill them. We just need to stop them until we can reach Hades.

I'm gonna crack their bones, disembowel them, and lay their innards inside out. Maybe, if I'm kind, Gorgiana, I won't dismember them for you.

I turn to their car. They now have both doors open and are using them to shield themselves.

My left arm is thrown back. I feel sharp pain. I look down and there's a smoking hole blown through my sweater sleeve. Blood and rain are trickling down my left hand. I grip my right hand, now made sharper with longer fingernails. I can't move my left hand.

"We just want the Mandrigel," someone shouts from the SUV. "Not you, Medusa. Then we'll leave your friends alone."

I growl. That sends them hiding behind their open car doors. I'm hit again. This time a bullet strafes my neck.

I've had enough.

I sprint to their car, grab the driver's door with my right hand, and tear the door off. I'm so fast that the Imada agent still has his gun pointed at Sandra's car. I tackle him to the ground before he can turn the gun on me. Then I thrust my right fist into his chest. I punch him hard enough to penetrate his ribs and make contact with the muscle that is his heart. I crumple his beating heart in the palm of my hand. It looks as if I dipped my hand into red Jell-O. His body lies on the ground shaking.

My hair is pointing behind me. One of the strands, fully grown into a thick viper, extends from my body and strikes at the other guy's head. It aims right for his sunglasses and penetrates his eyeball. Now that agent is screaming against the car door, his eye ripped out of its socket. The snake is finally satiated by eating an eye—not sure why my snakes have been wanting to do that so badly lately.

The final guy is in the front of the car. He's firing his fucking pistol like crazy at my back.

It hurts...so...bad.

He's in my grasp. I don't recall how he got there.

I'm going to rip his fucking head off!

But we only need to disable him. Medusa, like I was saying, there's no reason to kill—

His head rolls on the sand by my foot.

That leaves one guy: the agent still screaming on the ground, clutching his head, with a missing eyeball.

I rush him.

Don't kill him yet, Medusa!

I lift him up.

"Are any others following me?" I cry, holding him in my arms. But he won't stop holding his head in his arms, covering his eyes. "Tell me! Any others!"

I think he's in too much shock.

Just let me put him out of his misery.

No. Enough bloodshed.

I grab his hands from behind him. He's in too much shock over missing an eyeball to object.

I haul him to his SUV. I throw him on the passenger's seat, pin him down with my leg, and tear out the seat belt. I use the belt to tie his hands and then I tie him to the truck.

All done.

Then I head back to the BMW.

I take a deep breath because I'm panting like crazy. I open the door. I'm surprised to see Sandra sitting up straight in the passenger's seat, staring out the windshield at the incoming ocean waves, just like she was doing before I growled at her when I stopped the car.

"Are you hurt?"

She doesn't say anything. She just stares forward.

"Engel, are you still back there?"

"Sì."

"You okay?"

"Sì. But your friend is in shock, Guardian."

"So am I," I say with a sigh.

I plop back in the front seat and stare at the dark ocean waves crashing around the front of Sandra's car for a moment. My body's shaking. My heart's pounding. I'm soaking wet. It's not only rain, it's sweat. And blood. Holes in my left arm and neck are now bleeding profusely. And it burns...

I reach inside my pocket for my phone.

I text *Aner* with my right hand. I still can't move my other hand.

"We were in a fight. One Imada survived. I tied him to their SUV. The other two are dead. It's on the beach in Sunland by Mission Street."

"Leave the scene." It's almost an immediate response. *"Go home and DON'T leave your house again until we tell you it's all clear."* I reach back to put my phone away. But then I feel it buzz again. *"I didn't say it was safe to leave your house yet."*

I roll my eyes. Then I look back at Engel. He's sitting in the back seat. Oddly, he doesn't look bothered at all by the violence. But Sandra is completely frozen. Even when one of my snakes accidentally touches her shoulder, she doesn't pay any attention.

I consider whether to text him about Engel. I don't. Instead, I press down on the brake while pressing the ignition.

Sandra jumps. Then she screams. That scares the shit out of me. But then she just freezes again. And I hear what sounds like a chuckle from her. Have I driven her nuts?

Who knows. It could be an improvement?

Shut it, Medusa. Why'd you have to kill two of them?

I stopped them, didn't I?

Another buzz shakes my pocket. It's from *Aner*: "*Did you happen to see our Mandrigel?*"

I look back and Engel is still behind me.

"*No,*" I text back.

Why'd you do that?

All the gods want him, including the jerk. I need to talk to him first.

You talk too much.

6

THE ONE WHO SCORNS YOU

I RUSH OVER TO MY FRONT DOOR, JINGLE MY KEYS, AND OPEN IT. The only light emanates dimly from the living room.

"There you are," Asher says from the living room, where he's been watching TV. "I stopped by the restaurant after you didn't answer your phone. You were gone. Where'd you go?"

I fling some of the water off me by the door. I hear him get up and walk toward me. Then he freezes near the kitchen. He's not petrified by my eyes this time. It's my appearance. All my clothes are stained crimson with blood, and my sweater has a gaping hole in it.

"What the hell happened, Gorge!"

I follow his eyes to my left arm. There's blood dripping from my sleeve. I didn't even realize I was still bleeding. The pain's going away and the wound is closed.

"Are you okay?"

I shake my head. "Ash, don't worry about me. Your sister's still in the car. I'm so worried about her. She won't come out of the car. She's totally in shock. We had a car accident."

"She took you home? Why?"

"No. She was too drunk to drive."

He stares at my face in surprise. I quickly avert my eyes. "But you can't drive."

Yep. He looks over my shoulder and sees the car across the street. It's parked at a weird angle, in the pouring rain, but I don't think he can make out all the huge dents and broken glass yet.

"What happened?" he says again.

"Imada. They attacked us. But your sister was in such a state. I'm not sure if being drunk was a good thing or a bad one. She's so messed up now, Ash. She just broke up with Jack and the wedding's off. Then this happened."

"Oh, God."

"Yeah. Then we were shot at. Her car's wrecked. The doors and bumper are full of bullet holes. She's totally freaked out, but in a weird, quiet way. She's so quiet, it's unsettling. She vomited when we reached this neighborhood, wiped her hand, and then went back to staring through the windshield like nothing happened. Her clothes are covered in vomit, but she's too weirded out to care. I'm so worried about her, Ash."

"Was she hurt?"

"No, thank God. We were first attacked at the restaurant. Then they followed us to the beach, where I changed."

"Did she see you change?"

"Yeah."

He nods slowly.

"That's not all."

"I can't get her to leave her seat," interjects another voice.

I look down. A man the height of my waist with dark blue skin, thin white hair, baggy 1920s clothes, and wide shoes—also ancient looking—is looking up at us. I quickly shake my head.

Why are you here! Get out of here!

Ash lurches back and freezes again—and again, he isn't being petrified by my eyes. He's totally weirded out about the small blue dwarf under him.

"Who? ... What?" asks Ash. "Who is that?"

"My name is Engel." Engel reaches up his stubby hand to shake Ash's. Asher ignores his hand.

"I told you to stay in the car, Engel," I snap.

"I thought it'd be better if I came inside," he says. "Not for me, but for that woman in the car. There are still agents patrolling the streets. I need to hide indoors, away from her. I don't want to endanger her. I tried to talk to her, but it just made things worse. If you will permit me, Medusa, I'll stay in the house. After what happened, she doesn't want me anywhere near her."

Ash shakes his head hard. I don't think he's telling Engel no. I think he's just trying to process everything. Then he looks back outside at Sandra's car.

"Help me get her into the house, Gorgi," Ash says.

As we're walking back, the rain stops. Finally. That allows me to scan the area with my hair. But my hair's not the only thing searching the neighborhood. My head's snapping back and forth as my eyes scour the area.

"What happened to Sandra?" Ash asks again as we walk across the street. He grabs my left arm and I wince. It's the one with the bullet wound. "Oh, sorry."

"It's okay. I told you already. Your sister's seriously freaked out because she was in the middle of a gunfight."

"No, it's because she saw you transform," he says quietly. "Did ... did she see you fight them?"

I shake my head. "Well, I don't think she did. I ... I'm not sure. But you're right, I know she saw me change."

He nods again. "And that thing."

"That 'thing' is just a short man."

"With a blue face. I can see why he hides."

Before I can say anything else, we're at the passenger's door of Sandra's car. And, of course, she's still sitting in her seat just staring at nothing. Ash knocks on her window. She jumps and then throws the door open. It hits Ash, but she hardly seems to care.

"*What the fuck is wrong with you! Huh, Ash?*" Sandra hits his chest. Then she glances my way and shakes her head. "What kind of a girl are you going out with?"

"Medusa," I say.

"I mean, she's got fucking snakes in her hair!" Sandra says. "And fangs for teeth. She's a total monster. Did you know that? Did you?"

Yeah, he knows that. She gazes at me again. I look normal now, but my clothes are still stained red from blood.

I can change back if it will shut her up.

Shh. Quiet!

"*What* is she, Ash!"

"Medusa," I say again.

"What?" she cries, turning to me.

She looks down at her black blouse. It's wet and full of flakes of food from her vomit. I think she had forgotten she threw up. That only makes her angrier.

"Fuck! We almost got killed, Ash! What the hell's going on!"

"I'm Medusa," I say again, for like the fortieth time.

"*What about Medusa!*" Sandra shouts at me.

"I *am* Medusa, Sandra. I'm that mythical Greek lady with snakes in her hair. That's who I am. I was born in Sarpedon, Greece, a long time ago. I've been alive—"

"What?" Sandra asks. "What are you talking about? *Greece?*" She stares at my hair. It's normal, but I'm guessing she's remembering when it wasn't. "What the hell—"

She closes her eyes. Her head tilts. And she falls. With quick reflexes, I catch her in my arm—the uninjured arm.

It's a good thing. She was falling straight back and would probably have slammed her head against the concrete. I lift her and carry her into the house.

"I've never seen her like this," Asher says.

"She's drunk."

"I've never even seen her drunk," Ash says with a shrug as I carry her to my door. "Drinking, sure, but never drunk."

"She's not getting married, Ash. That, along with Imada almost killing her—and, of course, me—messed her up real bad."

Just when I think it can't get any worse, I find the small blue dwarf waiting for us inside the house by the threshold. That makes me thankful that Sandra fainted. He has a kind smile, but the look of him, a short man in wet, baggy clothes with glowing blue eyes and a blue face, has Ash looking peaked. And for a split second, I worry he's going to need to be carried too.

Instead he follows me as I carry Sandra down the hallway to my bedroom.

"Leave us alone," I say to Ash. "I'll change her in bed."

Ash nods and closes the door behind us.

I lay Sandra gently down on my bed. Her clothes stink of vomit and it's gross, but I'm too worried to care...sort of. The smell makes me want to throw up too. Outside the room I hear Ash trying to strike up a conversation with the dwarf, which, I suppose, in a different situation would be kinda funny. I pull off Sandra's stinky black shirt. Then I work on her shoes. I grab a robe and cover her with it. She's still a bit stinky, but I'll worry about washing it all later.

I hear a knock on the door.

"You need anything, Gorge?" It's Ash. I smell Engel, still standing by the kitchen.

"Yeah. Get me a bucket from the lower bathroom cabinet. And just put it by the door." I hand him her shirt and pants rolled in a ball. "Judging by how much she drank, she'll be throwing up again."

"All right."

Then I pull up my desk chair beside the bed. I sit in the dark with only dim light from my nightstand. After a moment, though, I jump up and grab a book from the desk. It's getting late at night, but this is morning for me. And after everything that's happened, I'm hardly tired. I'm hurting though. But the gunshot wound is healing, and the wound has closed. So it's time to engage in my favorite pastime. It'd be too dark for a human to read, but as you well know, I'm not human.

So I open my book. I used that antique cross my gorge boyfriend gifted me after we met to mark my place. It's my newest relic and I love it. It's my favorite.

This mass paperback is titled *From China with Love*. It's by the same writer who wrote *The Guy That Loved Me and Then Died*. They're supposed to be trashy romance Bond spoofs—*I think*. They're really awful. Awfully good, I mean. I'm not even sure if they were written to be funny, but they really are. I'm totally addicted. I love James Bond. Before Ash, I used to spend all my Friday mornings on the sofa, with microwave popcorn, binging on James Bond flicks. It was like a private singles' event. Then when I got my fill of testosterone, I'd turn to the *Titanic* or *Gone with the Wind*. Those are some great flicks too. Or I'd bawl my eyes out after watching *The Notebook* for the thousandth time. I'd sympathize really hard with Allie from *The Notebook* for not remembering her past. Because no matter how many times I watch stuff, I can't remember everything either. And I've lived a long life. You know, I think if we remembered everything in books and movies, things would become rather dull. What would be the point in seeing a movie all over again if you recalled every detail of every scene? But losing one's identity in the arms of everlasting love? Ohhh, *The Notebook*...fuck, that's a good tale. Still, I like the good ole suspense of Bond flicks even more. I mean, all Bond movies are amazing. Movies are probably the best invention of the twentieth century. Maybe they're the best invention ever.

Anyway, right now, the main spy, in a suit, is trying to pick up a really pretty Asian girl playing Baccarat with this devilish bald Asian lady who's the head of MSS. MSS is like China's CIA. They're playing cards really intensely. Turns out the girl he keeps eyeing is an MSS agent too. I know that from foreshadowing planted five chapters ago. So he's in it real deep. But probably not before some action—like in chapter three. And I don't mean "action" as in gunfire and explosions, if you know what I mean. I'm talking about the other kind of action I like reading.

Yummy.

But as I'm reading about another romantic hookup for our heroine, Sandra stirs in bed.

I touch my hair. It's down.

"Gorgi?" she asks, squinting up at me. She closes her eyes tightly, wincing at the light. The lamp light from my nightstand is actually really dim.

"Hi."

She turns to my window. There are no drapes. My bedroom windows are all boarded up. Over the centuries I've learned that sleep is a great time to accidentally reveal my identity, so I don't take any chances in my bedroom. No open windows where I sleep. Sandra furrows her brow staring at my boarded-up window because it's yet another thing she doesn't get about me. Then she turns toward the edge of the bed. She starts dry heaving. I quickly grab the bucket from outside the room. She hurls more vomit into the bucket.

Gross!

"You doing okay?" asks Asher from the hallway outside the door.

"We're fine," I say. "Just leave us alone, Ash."

"I feel like shit," Sandra groans. She rubs her mouth with the back of her hand. I lean her slowly back onto the pillow.

"You're just drunk. It'll pass."

"I don't think I ever drank so much in my life."

Wait a second. She's been drinking, right? Maybe I can convince her that I'm not you? Maybe she can believe that my changing and the gunfight were all a dream. I can convince her that I'm just plain librarian Gorgiana?

Yeah, sure. Good luck with that.

"My brother really knows how to pick 'em," she says.

"What?"

She's insulting me NOW? REALLY?

She looks into my eyes. Out of habit, I look away.

"You have beautiful eyes," she says. "I've always liked them."

"I hate my eyes."

"So, you're *Medusa*?" She knows it's not a dream. "Like *the* Medusa from mythology. With snakes in her hair?"

I nod hesitantly. You're right, with everything she witnessed, I won't even try to convince her it was a dream. Especially when she sees her car later.

"Did Ash ever tell you how much I hate snakes?"

And I hate you, bitch.

Shh!

I shrug and say, "Sorry."

"You saved my life." She takes my hand, still looking deeply into my eyes. "Thank you." She reaches her other hand up to my hair. "Your hair looks nice. Now."

One of my wigglies snaps at her finger, nearly biting it. It was buried inside my normal hair.

Why'd you do that! You could have hurt her!

I hate her! You might want to get lovey-dovey, Gorgiana, but I don't! We'll never be friends. She's a bitch! Stay away from her!

You almost hurt her! She's Asher's sister!

I should have bitten her finger off.

"I'm sorry, Sandra," I say, standing up. "I'm so sorry."

Sandra covers her eyes. She starts shaking. For a moment, I think she's seizing or something. But then I hear whimpering. She's crying.

"I'm so sorry, Sandra." I reach out, but she yanks her hand away and turns her back to me. "I don't always have control."

"This has to be the worst night of my life!" she says. "The worst! I catch Jack cheating on me, get dragged into a gunfight, and find out that my little brother is in love with a lady with snakes in her hair. I *hate snakes!*"

I sit back in my chair. Then I fold my arms and shake out the hair she hates. "I'm sorry I bit at you."

She chuckles. She actually laughs. Or is it crying?

"It's all an act, isn't it?" she says.

"What do you mean?"

"It's an act? This whole librarian thing. I always suspected it, ever since you performed at The Alcove. You weren't shy. Oh, no, you were someone else. Or something else. Even when you walk around with that ugly get-up of yours, you're not who you're trying to look like. You don't always fool people, you know. I've seen it. I was puzzled when I met your friend Cora. I didn't understand how someone so cool could like you so much. I've watched people just about to step on you, and then you come out ready to bite their hand off, just like you were about to do to me."

"I wasn't," I say again. "I just don't always have control."

"That's what the glasses are about, aren't they? And your hair in a bun? Gorgiana is all a disguise."

"No, I'm Gorgiana too."

But she laughs and shakes her head. "God, I don't know why I didn't see it before. I mean, you're so beautiful, even in those awful clothes you wear, but I never could get why my brother could be into someone so weak. Now I know. It's all an act."

"Your brother's the sweetest guy in the world."

"See," she says, suddenly very earnest. She looks right into my eyes again. I turn. "There it is. You're defending him with that bite of yours." I look back and she nods slowly. She squints right into my eyes. "What's with your eyes anyway? They don't look normal."

I cover them with my hand. "They're poison. The gold mesmerizes people. If I stare too long and they turn green, they turn people to stone. If I stare for a minute or longer, I can even turn *things* into stone."

"Medusa," she says with a slow nod.

"Medusa."

She nods again.

"Sorry," I mutter.

She looks away and shrugs.

Then it's quiet.

I sniff around. It stinks. I worry that the vomit is affecting me so much that I'm letting my guard down.

I'm being stupid. I haven't been smelling around the house for intruders all this time. Asher and Engel could be in trouble.

No, through a green image that appears in my mind, I smell Ash lying on the couch in the living room trying to sleep. But Engel is in the hallway near our door. Is he listening in on us? Why is he always snooping around? No doubt he has no idea I smell him. I'm ready to throw open the door and confront him, but then Sandra starts crying all over again.

"What's wrong now, Sandra?"

"Thank you for saving me," she says between tears.

"You don't sound very happy about it."

"I just lost my fiancé, 'kay?"

I lean in and hug her. I feel some of my wigglies ready to strike her. (I swear, if you touch her, I'll submerge my head underwater in the university pool all night tomorrow!)

But she smells sooo gross.

I wrap my arms tightly around her. And she cries in my arms.

"I feel so bad," she says.

"It'll work out. Just forget it. Forget everything and just rest."

"I thought he was the one, Gorgi. I really did. I really thought he was going to be the one I'd marry and love for the rest of my life."

I get that. You know, I recall so many men who I thought were the one. That's the thing about living for eons. You go through a lot of heartbreaks. And I came so close to marrying some of them.

One time, right before I walked down the aisle with this tall Irish guy in a church in Dublin—at night, of course—he took out a knife and tried to stab me in the heart. I mean, *literally* in the heart. But I hadn't told him about my invincible immortality yet. Well, my hair explained it to him afterward.

"It'll all work out," I say again quietly.

And then she falls limp in my arms. For a moment, my heart jumps all the way up to my throat in horror with the thought that my awful other half squeezed her to death. I didn't. She just fell asleep in my arms. All the stress must have exhausted her. So ever so gently, I remove myself from her grasp. Then I walk to the door.

Engel's in the hallway waiting. Watching. I put a finger over my lips and shush him.

"Why are you spying on me again?" I snap in a forced whisper. "Huh?" I gently close the door behind me. Then I kneel. "You shouldn't be eavesdropping. I saw you looking at me that first night too. And I know you saw what Ash and I were doing."

"I'm sorry," Engel says. "That night, I came here to meet you. Then I looked around your place for an entrance because Imada was following me."

"It was humiliating."

"And shocking."

"Yeah. I know!"

"No." He points to my hair. "Not the sex. I'm old, like you, Medusa. But I've never seen—" And he points at my hair.

"Just shut up about it, 'kay?" Then I look back at the door and think of Sandra. She and Ash are sleeping, and I'm getting riled up enough to glow green at Engel. So I say more softly, "But why are you snooping around now?"

"Arachne told me you were misunderstood. She said: lei è un mito. In English, that means—"

"I know what that means."

"Legendary," he says with a nod. "But when she called you that, she wasn't talking about myth. She meant that there is no other person like you. She said that you're thought to be the most terrible monster, but you're actually the best person with the greatest heart of anyone she has ever known. She said only you can be trusted. Now I see that she's right."

He reaches into an old leather bag on his belt and removes a small crystal jar the size of my hand. It glows scarlet under my hall light. Then he holds it out to me.

"I don't want it," I say, shaking my head.

"Take it, Guardian. You took Nephree's scepter. Now this, too, belongs to you."

"No." But I gaze at the small glowing ruby in his stubby blue hand. I can't resist holding it. It's beautiful.

"There is only a small amount left," Engel says, looking down at it. "Just drops—"

"It's so beautiful."

"Powerful enough to turn a mortal immortal when baked into ambrosia. Deadly if drunk in this liquid form. It's existed for three thousand years in the possession of my Amazon nymphs. The jar, the golden fleece, and the scepter have been guarded by my people for so many centuries. I've guarded it as best I could, but I didn't want it. Now you must have it. You shall be its rightful guardian. After all, that is what *Medusa* means in the ancient Greek tongue: Guardian."

"Engel, I'm a monster," I say, shaking my head. "I've killed innocent people. I've turned people to stone. Didn't Arachne tell you about that too? I've done terrible things. I have no right to such a thing."

"No. You're our Guardian. Arachne and I know it. Look how you just comforted a woman who scorned you." He points to the bedroom door. "I watched you in the restaurant. That woman in there is always mean to you. And now you comfort her."

"Sandra needs me tonight. She was going to get married and the wedding's off. She feels lost. I only help her because I'm in love with her brother, Ash."

"You comfort the woman who scorns you," Engel says with a gentle smile and a shake of his head. "That is the action of a queen. That is like my Nephrea. Nephrea did the same for your friend, Cora. Your friend Persephone is not a good person, Medusa. But Nephrea took care of Cora as if she were her daughter. Even before Nephrea went to save her, she raised her when Cora was young, rotten, and spoiled. Nephrea comforted one who scorned her too. Persephone. Just as you do today. If Nephrea were alive, I'd give the jar to my Nephree because it belongs to Amazon queens. But there are no Amazon queens left in the world anymore. So I hand it to you. Because you are of the same heart as one. That is why Cora and Arachne love you so much."

"Why not give it to Cora?" I try to hand it back to him. I'm still on my knees. Even on my knees I'm almost taller than him. "Persephone can protect it. She belongs to your family."

"I don't trust her. She destroyed my home, Medusa."

"What about Hades?"

Engel's eyes open wide. He is staring right into my eyes, so I quickly turn away. He violently shakes his head.

Remember what Cora said. Hades tortured Engel's people.

Yes, I forgot. No, Hades would be the last person Engel would trust.

"The jar belongs to you, Medusa," Engel says. "Take it. With my home buried under the sea, and all the Ambrosia queens dead, we can no longer guard it. We need you. We need The Guardian. Arachne trusts you. I trust Arachne. You guard the scepter, and now you must guard Pandora's Jar."

7

MY QUIET LIBRARY

I'M ROLLING MY BOOK CART DOWN AN AISLE OF BOOKSHELVES. It's early, so my library's still a bit noisy. I'm not a fan of my early shift. I've always been an eat-your-vegetables-before-dessert kind of girl, you know, so I tolerate the noise of girls using the cubicles to smooch or gossip because I know 6:00 p.m. is still early. But the bookworms that stay late are a lot easier to handle. I really feel bad for the day shifters. Really, I do. I don't know how my friend Maryann—she's got the day shift—has the patience.

Anyway, I'm shelving *Of Mice and Men*. Remember that book? Sometimes I totally identify with Lennie. (That's why I was so horrified last night when Sandra stopped moving in my arms.) I really love that novel. I bawl my eyes out every time I get to the ending—even though I've read it a couple times now. I won't give it away. Just have a large box of tissues nearby when you read it.

Hmm, here's a geography book on Africa I'm shelving in an upper row. I've memorized all the rivers of the continent. There are, of course, the Nile and Congo. But many people don't know about the Limpopo, Zambezi, and Cubango.

Shit, I even know the tributaries. I've learned lots of weird facts over the centuries.

I take an elevator down to our elegant main hall. Here there's a giant room with architecture from the nineteenth century. It's a huge hall with wood walls and a vaulted dome ceiling. Long chandeliers with pretty crystals hang over rows of large wooden tables.

Anyway, my route tonight, unfortunately, takes me along the long tables in the main hall, picking up books near a ton of students yapping who haven't gone to dinner yet. They're certainly not acting like they're studying. There are so many of them that I have to avert my eyes. Even when I pick up a book or trash, I have to make sure to not look at anyone. It's okay. Students rarely notice me.

Except Asher. Remember that first time?

Ahhh...that was so nice.

Wait... Don't you smell him?

Yeah, I do! Is he here?

"Gorgi?" It's Asher.

I whirl around. He totally looks like a student. He's got a backpack slung over a black T-shirt and jeans. His blond hair is combed but thrown to the side, as he always does. Cute—as always.

He takes me into his arms.

"Cut it out, Ash," I mutter quietly. "I told you not in public."

"Blowing your cover?"

I nod. And, wouldn't you know it, a bunch of students who had their heads in their books look up curiously from their table.

"We need to talk," he says.

"Now?" I reach up and brush my fingers over that long wave of hair on his head that I love so much. It's wet. It must be raining outside.

"It's real important."

"Okay." I nod and signal to the other side of the building. "Follow me."

"To the fountain?" he asks with a smile.

"Of course."

Mr. Handsome knows I love our library fountain. Yeah, it's my favorite spot. I love to read books in peace there. It's private, even at this time of day.

We walk down a few steps and sit down on them. Unless it's super crowded during finals week, students never sit on the steps. Then I gaze at the lovely trickling water.

"You know I'm working," I say quietly.

"I know, babe," he says. He sounds solemn and takes my hand. "I'll be quick. After last night, Sandra not only lost Jack, she lost her home. See, she was so ready to get married that she had moved in with him. That makes her homeless now. She's looking, but it'll probably take a week or so for her to find somewhere to stay."

"So you want her to stay with us?"

"Kind of." He nods. Then he looks at my face. He's so well trained that he manages to glance at me without gazing into my eyes. No man who hasn't been around me long enough can pull that off without being drawn to my eyes like a magnet. But Asher can.

But then he clams up.

"What?"

"Gorgi... I know how much the two of you don't get along. But I thought that since you planned to take Engel by car up to Toronto tomorrow, your house would be available. It'd be a helluva lot better than staying with my roommate at my apartment."

"I don't know."

"And Sandra's warming up to you, especially after she found out about who you are. It's weird. It's like she has a new respect for you. She always told me how cool she thought Cora was when Cora visited. Now she's starting to think you're cool like her. And she's convinced you saved her life."

"I don't care if she respects me, Ash. And I really didn't save her."

You kind of did.

I didn't.

You did. You actually stopped three goons from shooting her.

No, I didn't.

"Are you talking to yourself again?" he asks.

"What? How can you tell?"

"You sort of drift off. Look, Gorge, her car's totaled, her fiancé's gone. I'm thinking that if you leave town with Engel, most of our troubles should leave with you. Not to mention, Hades still guards your place, not mine. I think it'd be perfect for at least the next few days."

"Fine."

"Really?" He squeezes my hand. "Are you sure?"

"I kinda feel responsible for her car," I say with a shrug. "But, I mean, I really don't think I saved her life, I think I brought her trouble."

"She's going to appreciate this so much!" he says. "I don't even think she hates snakes as much anymore. Even after you pecked at her. She's that thankful. This will be so great, babe. So when you and I head to Toronto tomorrow—"

"Wait a minute. You, mister, aren't going with me." And I poke his chest. "I'm going alone."

"You don't even know how to drive," he says with a smug grin. "All you do is wreck cars."

"It's not funny. That was an emergency. This time, I can take a bus."

"I can study at Cora's," he says, shaking his head. "Plus I

love her place. I want to see Gabe and that little tyke too. Unless you want to take a plane. It's a long drive."

"Cora said the best way to stay incognito is for us to go by car. She said Imada's watching her movements and her private jet would only bring attention to us."

"Then we drive. It's settled."

I shake my head. He nods his.

"Ash, just stay with your sister."

"Engel thought I should go too," Ash says. "He said it's harder to disguise himself by car. He thought you might need help to keep him hidden. Or maybe he fears you being behind the wheel again." He laughs. "You're sure about lending your place to Sandra?"

"Yes."

He takes me into his arms again. Then he touches his lips to mine.

He comes closer. And he kisses me some more.

"Ash, stop," I say in a hushed whisper. "Not here." I pull back.

"I'm sorry, I can't help it." Then he gets up. But we're still holding hands. He slowly lets go of my fingers. "You don't know how happy you'll make Sandra. I'll be at your place in a few hours. I'm gonna meet upstairs with a study group for my anthropology class. Then we can pack."

"Well, you'll be staying with your sister at the house."

"Not if you want to use my car."

"I can steal it."

"Please don't. Sandra and I are already dealing with her insurance after the last car you destroyed. You don't know how to steal cars without ripping doors off."

"Stay at the house," I hiss. "Please, Ash!"

He laughs, all smug, and puts a finger over my lips to shush me. "Love you, babe. This is so incredible of you."

"*Guardian.*"

What... Who was that? That wasn't Asher. Was that you?

No.

I whip my head back and forth, searching. Then I stand up so I can look over the steps down the main hall. All I see is students quietly studying.

"Guardian."

Wait, I recognize that voice. It's... Engel's.

"What is it?" asks Ash.

"Don't you hear him?"

"Guardian."

Ash shakes his head.

"I need help, Guardian. I left your house because I was being pursued. They're all over campus and they're on their way here."

"Where are you, Engel?"

But I realize that, although I can hear him, there's no way he can hear me. I lift my head and sniff again. Then I scan all the shelves with my monster eyes. My mind sees two images—what my eyes can see and a green image, through all the walls, that is invisible to most people. But I can't locate him. This little fellow is way too good at hiding, this time to his detriment.

"They're outside," Engel says.

Ash stands up and looks around too, but if I can't find Engel, he sure won't. "What's wrong, Gorge?"

I snatch Ash's elbow and pull him down the steps. I catch two men wearing all black and shades coming up the escalator from outside the building. As I smell the agents approaching, I smell something else. It is lit green, at the far end of the hall, crouched in darkness. He has a blanket or sheet over him, but those bright azure eyes are peeking out.

"How far is your car?" I ask Asher.

"It's in a lot between Allie the gator and the Odeum."

"Shit, that's far."

"Why?" Ash asks. "What's going on?" He moves to walk up the steps again, but I yank him back down.

"Stay down! Ash, I think I have to take you up on your offer after all," I say. "Imada is moving up the escalator. No anthropology study group tonight. Okay?"

"Sure. Fine."

"But we need a diversion."

But what?

The fucking Imada are walking over to all the windowed walls of the library offices. Why? Do they think my boss, Charlie, knows where a small blue dwarf is hiding?

"*If you hear me, Guardian,*" Engel says, "*I'm letting them capture me now. I can't have them threaten the children.*"

Children? What children?

The college students are children to a four-thousand-year-old man.

I look at the huge, elegant floor-to-ceiling windows, beyond the aisles of books. They remind me of cathedral windows.

I shake my head without my control.

No Gorgi. No. No. NO!

"Ash, Engel is three aisles down from the restrooms to our right. Go get him out of the library and take him to your car as fast as possible."

"People will see him, Gorge."

"He has some kind of sheet over him. Gather him up in it and carry him."

I turn and shut my eyes hard. I have to fight all my will to not look into his eyes. Because I'm not thinking of him; I'm watching Imada and Engel, and my eyes are starting to shine like green flashlights. I turn and shut my eyes hard. I catch a student, who was studying at a table on the other side of the fountain, staring over at me.

"Gorge, your hair," Ash says. "You're changing."

Another three students, who were quietly reading at a table on the other side of the fountain, look over. My hair's not snakes yet, but it's moving. And my eyes are starting to illuminate everything in green light.

Gorgiana, I won't do it! It will hurt so much.

We need a diversion to save Engel.

Not that! Who cares about him?

If I'm fast enough, no one will see me.

"I'll meet you at the car," Ash says. Then he's off.

I look over at the windows. They're about the height of two people. And now I have to do what my worse half doesn't want me to do. Actually, I don't really want to do it either.

I swear, I'll trip. If you do this, I swear I'll fall and ruin everything!

"*Goodbye, Guardian,*" Engel whispers. He gets up in the aisle, removes the sheet covering him, and starts walking toward the main hall. "*If you can hear me, thank you for your care.*"

NO!

I shout so loudly that the word echoes in the old main hall. Then I let out a growl like a lion. All the students in the library turn. But before they have time to register who or what is growling, or take out their cellphones to snap a stupid photo of my stupid head, I'm running. I leap the three steps with one jump and hurdle over a long wooden table. I'm moving so fast that I see students slowly turning their heads. At this speed, they seem frozen in time. I'm in full-speed mode, dodging a chair, a backpack, a student with a backpack traipsing across the room, and then landing headlong into an aisle of books.

Shit!

Oops. That aisle's going down.

I run down another aisle. And then...straight through a very large glass window.

Straight...through...a large...fucking...hard...*solid*...glass window. As usual, it shatters, but it feels like solid stone. It fucking hurts.

Why do I always have to go through windows?

Now I'm airborne, hurtling two-and-a-half stories from the building.

I land crouched on my feet. I shake my head, trying to shake off the pain. Then I growl. This time I'm not being a beast; it's from sheer pain from the fall.

I whip around. I was so fast that there are no agents yet investigating the broken window. But they're coming. I see them, in the green map of the library in my head, rushing toward the exploded glass, while the love of my life is running in the opposite direction to fetch Engel. All this is happening so fast that Engel is still heading to the end of the book aisle.

I pull a shard of glass from my arm. Blood spurts all over the place. I think that one pierced an artery. My face is burning from scrapes, and blood is dripping down my sweater in the rain. I know it's blood from my lip and forehead because I taste salty metal and smell blood.

I growl again.

Because it hurts so bad!

Two students were walking down a walkway with an umbrella. And another guy with a backpack was rushing through the rain with a jacket over his head. They were heading in my direction. Not anymore.

Bang!

I'm thrown to the ground. I feel a piercing, sharp pain in my back. I think those assholes shot me.

I smell both agents, finally, crouched by the window.

They have their pistols drawn and are firing at me from the blown library window. Everything turns dark…

I wake up lying on the ground. Then I scream in pain again. My leg has a sharp pain. Now it's my back.

There are more cracks. They won't stop firing!

Get up, Gorgi! Run!

I limp my way to an adjacent cement walkway. The rain's pouring so hard now I can barely see. That's good. It'll mean fewer students will see me too. Using the strength of my left leg, I drag my whole body as fast as I can across a muddy grass field. With my right leg still whole, I'm moving at the speed of a runner, but with my lame leg I hobble. I probably look like a sprinting Quasimodo. They nearly blew my right arm off; it's dangling from my shoulder.

My phone buzzes. I reach for it in my pants pocket. That makes me scream in pain because I reached for it with my right arm.

Let me at 'em! Turn back!

There's no time, Medusa. We have to draw them away from Asher and Engel.

My phone buzzes again. I reach in my pants pocket with my left hand this time. The contact reads *Aner*: "Imada's searching your library."

No shit.

I leap down a hillside. This isn't the same spot where Ash and I hid; it's another muddy hill. There are lots of these swampy areas between buildings on campus. I roll halfway down the hill, until I hit a tree. The impact against my body hurts so much that—

Hi. Blacked out again.

Bang. More gunfire. *Bang.* Guess they're not bothering to talk this time. They're at the top of the hill, but they're shooting like crazy. If I were human, one shot would kill me. But they know it won't. It'll just knock me out. Are they planning to capture me?

I'm dragging my body through mud and branches under the cover of the undergrowth. When I reach the bottom of the hill, I make a run for it again. Or a running limp. Then I'm rolling down more muddy hills.

And now, finally, when I know I've lost Imada and drawn them away from Asher and Engel, I turn and race back as fast as I can. I'm heading back in the direction of my pursuers, but I take a parallel route, away from them, in the swamplands. Wiping the water from my eyes, I keep running, enduring the pain. I can't black out or they'll find me.

After forever, I see the parking lot across campus Asher was talking about. I call him. "Ash, quick, I'm...near your car. Come here and pick me up by the side of the road. Fourth Street."

"What took you so long?"

I answer by panting.

"You all right, Gorge?"

No.

I see his truck's headlights turn on in the parking lot. I turn around and search for the agents hunting me. I lift my nostrils and smell. They're far behind me, making their way down a muddy hill in the opposite direction. It's a faint green picture in my head, faint due to the pounding rain.

Ash's pickup drives on the shoulder of the road. He reaches over and throws open the passenger's door. "Jesus, Gorgi!" he exclaims, looking at me.

"Just go! Move it!"

I'm pushed back in my seat as Ash's wheels squeal and

skip along the wet asphalt. The pressure against the seat hurts like hell.

"Now I get the delay," Ash quips. "God, Gorgi."

Blood is everywhere. I move as close to his door as possible to limit the mess in his car. I groan. I hurt so much. Then I jump in surprise when someone touches my arm. It's a stubby hand. Engel's. His hands are a darker blue than the rest of his body. Now his fingers seem to be examining my arm.

"The other one's far worse," I say. "It's not whole."

"We should drive you to the hospital," Engel says. "You've been hit everywhere."

"I'll heal."

I take a deep breath and shut my eyes for a moment. I squeeze my eyelids tight. Before it was taking all my will to keep my eyes open. Now I want them shut. I just want to sleep. Rest. Maybe wake up in some gas station or diner, in another hour, when all my wounds have healed.

"It'll just take time, Engel. Thank you."

"Like Arachne?"

"Yeah, like Arachne," I say, looking back, forcing a smile at Engel. He's sitting in the back in the shadows. The back seat looks huge with his small body. "At least we have you. Do you have the jar, Engel?"

"No, it's at the house. I left it with you."

My phone buzzes. I scoot up. That feels terrible. Then I reach in and grab my buzzing phone from my pants. It's *Aner.* "*We'll detain them on campus. Leave. Highways are clear.*"

"Should I take you back to your house?" asks Ash.

"Hades says to just go. Get us on the freeway, Ash."

"Toronto?"

"Toronto. For Engel."

Then I squeeze my eyes so tightly. I'm breathing so heavily. And even shutting my eyes hurts from all the slashes and cuts on my cheeks.

"Sorry, Ash," I say.

"For what?" Ash asks. "Are you kidding me? Just tell me what to do to make you feel better, babe."

But I say nothing. Just...hoping for quiet. Stillness. Rest. And...

I reposition myself, waking up in pain, I think a few minutes later. I have every intention of letting my body drift off for hours. I just hope all the bullets went all the way through. When they get stuck, they sting like crazy when they're pried out.

"Thank you, Guardian," Engel says quietly behind me.

8

IT ONLY GETS WORSE

I OPEN MY EYES IN DARKNESS.

Then I'm thrown to the side of the car toward Asher, then swung back the other way against the car door. There's the squeal of brakes. The crash of metal.

What the hell's going on!

Asher is struggling with the steering wheel.

Outside I see only faint scattered lines by the center of the road; the rest of the road is hazy since it's pouring down so hard. I marvel at how Ash has been driving at all. Then I see the reason for the collision. A large SUV, you know, the one those Imada goons use, is inches from my side window. No, not inches, actually—

Crash.

The car shimmies back and forth as Ash struggles to control the wheel. I'm starting to light up the car emerald green, but with the pouring rain, I can barely see beyond the glow through the windows. I hear a grunt behind me. I think that's Engel. Yeah, I turn and Engel is braced against his passenger's seat holding his seat belt. Behind him, through the pouring rain, are four more headlights.

Crash.

I'm thrown forward against my seat belt. And that hurts like shit as it jars my still-aching arm and chest. Ash utters something incomprehensible. Then the truck on the passenger's side collides with us again. There are explosive sounds. But this isn't metal denting, it's gunfire.

The back window of Ash's car is blown open. Then pouring rain and wind rush inside the cabin.

"Pull over!" I cry.

"Gorgi, haven't you been hurt enough?" Ash exclaims.

"Just pull over!"

I don't care. I'm going to charge them.

But I'm thrown forward again as the car squeals its brakes. The guys in the SUV on our left overshoot us and drive around our truck, forcing us to slow down. My hair, now slithery, thick snakes again, looks behind me, staring at the other SUVs trailing behind.

"Pull over now, Ash! And then stay down for cover."

He can't. There's a burst of repetitive cracks. The car's swerving all over the road now. Judging from the way it's sliding, they probably pierced the tires with bullets.

The truck flips. It lands backward. Now we're sliding upside down across the road. Through the windshield, I see bushes and trees heading straight for me. Upside down. And then...

Shit, I blacked out again. I open my eyes, hearing more gunfire, but it's not our truck. I think there's another gunfight behind us.

"Are you all right, Ash?" We're hanging upside down in the SUV, dangling from our seatbelts. His eyes are still closed. "Ash? Ash!"

The truck shakes. It's upside down. My hair's smelling everywhere for the culprit. There's a guy in a black suit with shades brandishing a pistol. He's coming through the blown-open window in the back seat. He reaches for Engel. Engel undoes his seatbelt, falls on the ceiling, and stabs the guy's pistol-holding hand. The agent falls back and curls up against the metal ceiling of the car. Engel lunges again, this time at the agent's neck. The knife must have pierced an artery because blood spurts everywhere. Then the guy drops to the ceiling, motionless.

Engel's panting. He slides out the blown-up back window and looks around, still holding his small dagger in the pouring rain.

Another agent rushes him. I'm still making my way to the back of the truck. Then, a couple feet from me, the old dwarf slices the agent's ankles beneath his legs. The Imada agent falls, screaming in pain. Then Engel stabs this one's neck too. Now two agents are dead in the pouring rain. And all this happened in seconds. He is as fast a monster as I am; I didn't even have time to help him. It's a good thing. There's no way I could have gotten to him in time.

I stand outside with Engel in the pouring rain. Then I worry about Ash.

"Do you see any more coming?" Engel asks, searching everywhere. He's shielding his eyes from the pouring rain, searching the freeway.

"How the hell did you just do that? You killed them almost quicker than I could have."

"I know how to fight. I've been in war. Do you see any more of them?"

I scan the area. There are flashes of yellow light, back and forth, among my green schemata of the highway. And I hear loud cracks between black SUVs in the rain. I guess some of them are Imada, some are on our side. I can't tell.

Their scent is faint due to all the rainwater. Fortunately, aside from a nearby truck that belonged to the two dead Imada, the battle is happening about a quarter of a mile away.

"I only see fighting from those cars." I point at the flashing lights.

Engel nods.

Asher gets out of the truck. Thank God, he looks all right.

"Are you okay?" I ask.

"I'm fine, Gorge. What about you?"

"I'm fine, Ash. Fine."

"Engel?" Ash looks down.

Engel nods slowly, still staring at the far-off flashes of gunfire.

"How long was I asleep?" I ask. My right arm is back in its socket, but my back, arms, and legs are still burning.

"I didn't want to wake you," Ash says. "You were out for over half an hour."

"Can you turn the truck over, Guardian?" Engel asks. "We can at least use it as shelter."

I look down at Engel, but he knows not to gaze into my glowing green eyes. Under green light, he seems so intense. I have to say, I've been in a ton of battles myself over the millennia, but I haven't seen fighting like that. I don't think I'll ever understand this guy.

I walk over and lift the car, turning it over easily. My adrenaline is revved and I'm ready to toss the truck at someone. When it's right side up, we all quickly get inside for shelter from the pelting rain and sit back in the same seats —only I'm getting hit by dripping water through holes in the shattered glass. Then I lean my head against the passenger's door and try to sleep off more pain.

My cellphone shakes in my pocket. I'm surprised to see that it's not "Aner." It's Sandra.

"Hey, Medusa." She calls me Medusa now. It's her thing.

"Yeah, Sandra?"

"What's the matter? You don't sound too hot. I tried to call Ash, but he wasn't answering. Aren't you two coming home tonight?"

"It's Sandra," I tell Ash. "Sandra, we left tonight instead of tomorrow. We would have called, but we were chased by Imada on campus again. Now we just got chased on the freeway."

"Oh god. Are you guys okay?"

"Yeah." I heave a big sigh. "Fine. How about you? Are you safe at home?"

"Yeah. Never better. Listen to this. You won't believe it. Cora's swung by. Can you believe that? She suggested we go clubbing tonight. I suggested The Alcove. She said she's never been. I was thinking we could all go. I think getting out'll do me some good. I can't sit here forever thinking about you know who. I have to move on. You were right about that. And I love that you helped me, I so appreciate it, but staying at your house is driving me crazy. I can't be happy alone like you. Anyway, I found a temporary apartment for next week. I think..."

She's yapping and carrying on and on while I'm starting to feel really short of breath and sick.

"Sandra," I interrupt, "how can Cora be there with you?"

"Isn't it great! I was surprised too. I thought you were coming up to see her in Toronto tomorrow? Were you planning on seeing her here instead when you get back?"

You know that cliché where your heart drops to your toes and you feel ready to barf? Or your hair sticks up in total fright? Well...I feel both of them. And, actually, that second cliché is really happening. And my hair ain't pretty.

"Sandra. That's not possible. We're going up to Toronto to see Cora. She can't be there with you now."

"What are you talking about?" Sandra says with a laugh. "Cora met me at the Grotto when I was shopping for dinner. I showed her to your place. She's in your room right now."

Cora's in my room? In Florida? Did...she come down when she heard about the attack? But then, why wouldn't she call me? And, with all our trouble, why would she want to have fun?

She said she didn't want you to use the phone. Maybe she's trying not to alarm Sandra.

No. She would have called. Something's not right.

"What's she doing in my room right now, Sandra?"

"Rummaging through your stuff. She's desperate to find something she said you lost. First she glanced at all your relics in the living room. Then she said she had to check your bedroom. She said she's looking for something real important."

"And she looks like Cora? Like Cora when you met her? You're sure?"

"What?" Sandra laughs. "Medusa, it's Cora. She's got the same pretty bright blue eyes and long blond hair. The same face...or, well, it was dark and crazy back in the Euphoria nightclub, but she's her... You're starting to scare me."

"Sandra, listen carefully. Get out of the house. Get out now. Leave. Don't talk to *Cora*. Leave."

Ash stops working his phone and stares at me. Engel stands up right behind my shoulder.

"Why?" Sandra asks with another laugh.

"That's not Cora."

There's a pause on the line. My hand grips tightly. I'm glad it's not the hand holding the phone. I would have bent or cracked it.

"What's wrong, Gorgi?" asks Asher.

"What do you mean, it's not Cora?" Sandra asks, almost in a whisper. "What are you talking about?"

"I just don't think it's her, Sandra."

"God, we've been through so much shit this week, Medusa, I tell you, unless Cora has a twin, it's her."

"What's wrong?" asks Engel behind my shoulder.

I hear a loud thud on the other end of the phone. Then the sound of glass shattering.

"*Hey, what the hell are you doing?*" cries Sandra. "*Stop that!*"

"*Where is it! Tell me! Where is it!*"

"Sandra? Sandra!"

Click. The call drops. Then my eyes fill the truck with emerald light again.

"What's the matter?" asks Engel.

"Sandra said Cora's at my house," I reply. I shake my head hard. "It's not right. Then she hung up after some disturbance. It's impossible. Cora would have messaged me. She told Sandra they'd go to The Alcove. Cora might not know exactly what's happened, but even she's not going to go party it up now."

I look back at Engel. He's sitting deep in the back seat again. He nods contemplatively.

"An imposter," Engel suggests.

"I've been texting Triple-A," Ash says. "Unfortunately, we're in the middle of nowhere, getting absolutely nowhere. We need a tow. I can't even get any reception in this storm. Or my phone broke in the crash."

"She's in trouble, Ash," I say. "I just know it."

Gorgi, who cares about that bitch. She said she was looking through our relics. My relics, Gorgi! Whoever it is, she could take or break them!

I know, Medusa. I know.

"We need to go back," Engel says.

I nod.

But how? The rain's pouring. A lot of it's dripping loudly inside the car. I almost feel like I should get a pail. Ash's car is so totally totaled that water's coming in through the ceiling. I mean, it's a complete wreck. We don't need a tow; we need to ditch Ash's car and hitch a ride.

So I do what my best friend told me not to do. I dial Cora's number. It rings. And rings. And...

"Cora?"

"Gorgi, I told you not to call right now."

"Why are you at my house?"

"What?"

"Sandra said you're at my house. Is that true?"

"No."

Shit.

All my relics!

Quiet. Shut up.

But, Gorgiana—

"I heard from Hades about the gunfight tonight," Cora says. "I think this is it, Gorge. I think it's all coming down to tonight. You know those premonitions I get every night? I think it's all..."

I love Cora and all but I'm not listening to her. I'm staring at the drops of rain dripping down my passenger's window. We're not moving, but the rain is a useful distraction from the things spinning in my head. I'm doing everything I can to not think about my house and about all my—

Relics!

No, Sandra.

"What did Sandra say?" Cora finally asks. She stopped yapping after a while, after noticing I wasn't listening to her.

"She said you came to visit me." I heave a sigh. "That you're looking for stuff in my room. Cora, if it's not you, she's messing with all my stuff. All my relics, Cora. And Sandra."

"It's the jar. Whoever it is, they're looking for the jar."

"But Sandra said she looks like you. How?"

"Could be an Imada agent," Cora says. "Tell me. Honestly, please, Gorge, is Engel with you now? Please tell me."

"Yes."

"Put him on the phone."

He's still standing behind me. I hand the cellphone to him. Then I gaze out the cracked windshield behind him. I smell for any new intruders. Nothing. Of course, it's still pouring rain and hard to tell. And my eyes are still shining like a green beacon because I'm totally freaked out.

My boyfriend looks awful too. He has his head in his hands, rubbing his eyes. I reach over and rub his neck.

"No," says Engel behind me on the phone. "No."

God, Engel must really hate Cora. They haven't spoken in, like, a century and he's barely saying a word. He just grunted "hello."

"I hoped they'd catch me instead," Engel says.

"I'm so sorry, Ash," I say quietly, massaging his neck. "I'm sorry."

"Stop apologizing, Gorgi," he snaps. And there's an edge to his voice this time. "I told you, your problems are my problems. I'm just so worried about Sandra right now."

"I know."

"Are you still in pain?" He turns. He looks at my arm, while avoiding my gaze.

"Almost better."

"Possibly," Engel comments into my phone.

"We should have gone back when he said he didn't have the jar," I say. "I wasn't thinking about Sandra. That was so stupid."

Engel gets up from behind and hands me back my phone.

"If you're not there, Cora," I say, quickly grabbing the phone, "who is? Sandra said that if it's not you, it's your twin. Do you have some twin I don't know about?"

"We have ideas. That's why I spoke with Engel. But we're not sure. It doesn't really matter, does it? What matters is—"

"Sandra. She's in a lot of trouble. Can you help us?"

"Of course. Actually, I'm already flying down. I should be there in another half an hour."

"You're coming down?"

"Yes. And you need to head back to your house. I spoke with Hades and told him the problem's down there, not up here."

"But Cora, you have to guard your house. You have to care for Moros and Gabe. You should turn around. This could be a trap again."

"No, all the danger is centering down in Florida, in Sunland. And now it's endangering your friends, Gorgi."

"Can you get us a ride? Ash's car is a wreck. We're at the side of the road. Can you pull some strings and get us back to Sunland?"

"The car's totaled?"

"Yeah."

"I'll call Hades back," Cora says. "Stay on the road. I'll arrange for him to pick you up."

"How will he know where we are?"

"You can't be far from the gunfight, right? Things are coming down to tonight. Whatever Imada has planned, tonight's the night. And, sorry to say it, Gorge, it's right in your neighborhood again. Actually, not your neighborhood, your house."

"I know. Bye, Cora."

"Bye. I'll meet you there."

"They're coming to pick us up," I say to Asher the minute she hangs up. "We'll have to leave your truck."

"The truck's gone," he says with a nod. He glances at me. "I don't care."

"I know, babe. We'll get to Sandra as soon as we can."

Ash nods solemnly. I turn around and say to Engel, "What imposter could be at my house?"

"That's what Persephone asked me," Engel says. "There's one possibility, but no one's seen her in over a century."

"Who?"

My phone buzzes in my jeans pocket, and I check it. It reads "Aner." That's weird. He told me to never call, just text.

"Where's Engel?" Hades snaps.

"I thought you said to never call you?"

"Where is Engel, Medusa?"

"Here in the car with us. We're on the highway about an hour—"

"I know where you are. I didn't know if the little blue troll was there in the car with you. Answer me two more questions. Answer pointedly, if you want a ride. Why didn't you return to the house when you found out Engel didn't have the jar with him?"

"I don't care about the jar, I—"

"Injudicious. Is the scepter with you?"

"It's at the house."

"Ah." He sighs. "Of course it is."

"Look, I don't work for you, motherfucker."

"Thank the heavens you don't work for me, Medusa. You were given the simple responsibility of guarding two things, Guardian. The little rat and spider call you The Guardian. What kind of a guardian are you anyway?"

It grows silent. Ash looks over and furrows his brow.

"Look, are you picking us up or not?" I snap.

"Only because my bait is with you," he says. And he hangs up the phone.

A car honks its horn behind us. I can barely see its headlights in the torrential rain. It comes closer. It's another black SUV.

"Friendly or unfriendly?" asks Asher.

"If they were Imada," Engel quips, "they'd already be shooting at us, Asher."

The horn honks again. Then Hades's voice says from a megaphone, *"Why are you not leaving your car, Medusa? I thought you were in a hurry?"*

9

BACK HOME

WE'RE BARRELING DOWN THE HIGHWAY AND NOTHING'S stopping us. Blue and red are reflecting off my passenger's window and a siren is blaring. Cars are constantly pulling over or rushing by. In front of me, in the SUV, an agent in black and gray military camouflage is driving the car. And Hades is in the passenger's seat wearing green military fatigues. Engel is in the center seat, and Ash is to my right. But it's raining. No, not really raining. With the torrential rain, it's more like a hurricane. The SUV is swerving in the wind.

"And how are you, Engel?" asks Hades. We've been driving for nearly half an hour. We're probably almost back. This is the first time the bastard god has said a word. "It's been too long."

Engel doesn't respond.

"It's fortunate you're still alive," Hades continues. "Remarkable. An incredible feat for such a fragile little man. I am equally astounded that you were able to evade detection underwater in those caves. Tell me, because I've been dying to know, were you intimate with the spider lady in her underwater den?"

"You're such a pervert!" I snap.

"Haven't you been wondering, Medusa?" he asks with a laugh.

"No, I haven't. Don't answer him, Engel."

"It's a funny thing about you, Medusa," Hades says. "For thousands of years, you've been sticking your serpent head into things that really aren't your business. You really don't know when to mind it. You'd be far happier if you ignored everyone and kept your nose in books."

"Medusa is The Guardian," says Engel.

"I'm not," I say.

"So true, purple friend," Hades says. "Once, Gorgo, your lovely serpent head was displayed on Alexander's shield. You protected whole legions of men. But you also have always oddly suffered from low self-esteem. Well, now it's justified. You failed. You lost what you were guarding, didn't you? The Guardian wasn't able to guard a thing."

Hades turns around and smirks at me. He makes sure to look right into my golden eyes—because he knows he can.

I show him my middle finger.

"I'm sure your relationship, Engel, with the spider lady was completely platonic," Hades says with a laugh. Then he sinks back into his seat. "You and that librarian over there have a lot in common in your ho-hum monotony. I'm glad you two finally met each other. I'd think you'd get along quite well."

"I was surprised to see you pick us up in a car, Orcus," I remark, folding my arms. "It's not your style. I was expecting a helicopter."

"The nearest military base from me at the time of Kore's call was much further than your wreck. If you wanted to see your lover's sister, I realized we wouldn't have time. Not to mention the weather."

"We still might not be in time," I say.

"Yes, if the agent in your snake pit wants the subject dead, she's dead."

"Agents," I correct him. "There could be many Imada agents there. And try to at least *act* sensitive. That person you're calling a *subject* is Asher's sister."

"There are no Imada in Sunland," Hades said. "I can assure you of that. The mission was a success. We removed them. There are no communications, and there's no evidence pointing to them converging in your precious little college town. This imposter of Cora is not Imada."

"Then who is she, Hades?"

"I don't know, Medusa." He turns to the driver. "Tyler, how much longer? I need you to move faster."

"A few minutes, Orcus." The driver turns. "I'm moving as fast as I can. We're entering the city. But, goddamn, this wasn't a good time for a fight. The storm is picking up and is turning into a hurricane."

"I differ in opinion, captain," said Hades. "The timing of Medusa's home invasion is superb. Actually, it's a bit coincidental. We fight Imada, the imposter searches for treasure. Seems opportune."

The driver nods.

Through splashing rain, I recognize Sunland's Main Street. The water is splashing along the sidewalk, and the tires of a couple parked cars are submerged. Palm trees are swaying like crazy. I even see a car's fender under water. The driver's right: there's no one walking the street, even though normally there'd be students, even this early in the morning, walking around my college town. I think anybody's umbrella would be blown away.

"Turn right," I say.

"Tyler knows where your house is."

"Yeah? Been there before? Spying on me?"

He doesn't reply.

After a few more turns, we drive along my narrow college street to my quaint house. My patio is flooded. I jump when I see lights flickering on and off through the window. There could be a skirmish happening there now! I feel my fingernails lengthening. But before I tear the door open, as we stop at the curb, I see the strangest thing. A very drenched black McLaren, now submerged in water, is parked by the curb. And standing beside it is a blond woman wearing a black leather jumpsuit and holding a giant gray umbrella. The wind whipping around is strong enough to throw her, but the umbrella and her body are perfectly straight. That's because she has the strength of ten women. I'd recognize her and her car anywhere. It's Cora!

Cora runs to my door and takes me in her arms. I forget that this could be the fake Cora and let her gather me up in the rain. But then I step back cautiously.

"Gorgi, I'm so sorry this is happening to you and your friends." Now I know how Ash feels when I say that.

"How do I know it's you?" My green eyes scrutinize her face.

"It's me." Cora smiles wryly.

Ash runs to Cora's drowning sports car and hugs Sandra under the pouring rain. The passenger's door opens and I see Sandra. She looks fine.

Cora and I rush over.

"That woman," Sandra says to me, practically hyperventilating, "that... *other* Cora, whoever she is, is destroying your home, Medusa. She's mad. I... I just went to the Grotto to shop late for dinner. She met me and acted just like Cora. I mean...she sounded a little funny, but she looked and acted just like her. Then when I led her back to your house, she rushed straight to your room. That's when you called. And that's when it started. She started throwing and breaking things. It started small, but then she hurled whole bookshelves, your TV, anything and everything she could get her hands on. She broke things into pieces, and then scrutinized even the broken pieces. She even crumbled your brick fireplace, breaking the stone with her bare hands into dust. I ran. I was surprised she let me go. I ran outside and just stood in the pouring rain. But she's still tearing down your house."

"I had her go in my car for shelter," Cora explains to Ash and me, standing over Sandra, who is sitting on the sidewalk. Ash embraces Sandra again. "I caught her by your front door. It was just moments ago. But she was hysterical. I think she thought I was whoever it is who's ransacking your place, so I had to stop her from running. I just got here too."

"This is so you, Kore," Hades says standing over us. I didn't notice him come up. He's wearing a long black coat with a hood over his head. "Only you would drive a McLaren in a hurricane."

"It was either that or my motorcycle," she quips with a shrug.

Hades gestures to my house. "Shall we, my dear? Or have you already beat us to it?"

"I haven't gone in yet," Cora says, shaking her head.

There's a crash. I hear glass shatter. Great timing as we are all looking at my house.

My relics. Oh my God, my irreplaceable relics!

At least Sandra's okay.

Who cares about the bitch! They're priceless, Gorgi! Whoever it is, I'm going to shred her flesh, break every bone, and cut her to fucking pieces.

"Gorgi," Cora says, grabbing my shoulder, "I need you

inside with us. Only you know where you hid the scepter and jar. But—"

Three more black SUVs pull up to the side of the road. A few doors are thrown open, and men in green camouflage uniforms jump out. A few have machine guns strapped to their shoulders. Maybe it's a good thing that it's raining so hard? I can just imagine the attention this would get from all the students in Sunland on a clear evening, even in the middle of the night. But if they were seen, they'd probably be mistaken for national guard deployed due to a state of emergency over the weather.

"Ash, Sandra, stay outside," Cora says to my friends. Then she turns and looks down. Engel is beside her. She kneels beside him. "Engel. Engel, you stay outside too." Cora reaches out and takes his hand. She kisses the back of it. "I've tried to make things right."

"I know, Persephone. You've told me before."

"Enough sentimentalities, Kore," Hades says, still gazing at the house. "Whoever is impersonating you is ready to take the whole house down. For Medusa's sake, if she still wants a home, I suggest we go inside."

"Ash," Cora says, pointing to the soldiers, "you and your sister stay behind the soldiers. Stay far from the house."

"Not sure my men can protect them," Hades says, with his hands on his hips, still staring at my house.

There's a large crash and more glass shatters.

10

THE IMPOSTER

Hades, Cora, and I run to the front door. I break it open. I hear a lion's growl. That's me. Sandra wasn't kidding. My house is completely wrecked. I don't see a single thing that's not been tossed, turned over, or torn apart. Even the carpet's been pulled out and the floor has been dug up in places. My head whips to the living room with the force of my hair, fully thickened, smelling in that direction. Then I look at the fireplace mantle. And it's... It's... It's completely destroyed. That means my belongings spanning centuries...

Gone! All my relics are gone! Oh, my God, ALL MY RELICS! Where is she! I'm going to tear her apart!

I growl again.

Hades and Cora pay no attention. But their eyes are fiery red. Yeah, with their red eyes and my green ones, it's fucking Christmas at Medusa's house.

We walk to what was once my living room. Standing there with arms folded, leaning against the wall beside my broken window, is a woman. She has long hair and shiny red eyes. And wearing a T-shirt and jeans, dusty and torn, she is the spitting image of Cora, who is standing beside me.

"Where is it?" She squints at all three of us. I've never heard her voice. Or...have I?

"Mother?" asks Cora. "Mother, is that you?"

"*Where is it!*" the stranger snaps, pushing off from the wall. "I'm not here for a fucking reunion. Where's Pandora's Box? Tell me quick!" Then she turns her fiery eyes to me. "You have it, don't you, Gorgon? I found the scepter you hid." She shows it hidden under her right sleeve. "It was buried in your closet. The jar can't be there. There's nothing left of your room."

MY RELICS, Gorgi!

"*You bitch! None of this was yours!*" I snap. "*You ransack my fucking house!?*"

"Actually, Gorgo, the scepter and the jar belong to me," the lady says. "According to the laws of primogeniture. I'm older than my brother. And in many ways, since Zeus is gone, everything, including this staff, belongs to the goddess Demeter. Me."

"Sara," Hades says, "I should have known the imposter would be you. So good to see you. When was the last time?"

"Alamogordo, New Mexico. I told you back then we should have taken control of the world. You refused. That's when I knew never to offer an olive branch to you again." She turns to me again. "I can start digging, Medusa. Is that where you left it? Is it under the foundation of the house? Need I break that too?"

"Why do you want it so badly?" Cora asks.

"I wish to take it from you, daughter. You know your own prophesy. Such a thing shouldn't be in anyone's possession —most importantly, yours."

Sara comes a little closer. I marvel at her similarity to Cora. Cora's mother is like a mirror image of her. This was obviously purposeful to fool Sandra. She can match her daughter's appearance because, once the gods turn Cora's apparent age, they stop ageing. I think she thought this plan would work and she'd easily steal my stuff and just go. Well, I'm as good at hiding things as Engel is at hiding himself. That's the other reason Arachne trusts me with her stuff.

"I heard about what you three did to my niece." Sara laughs. "And poor Hermes. Do you think you can do that to me?"

"Why would we need to?" asks Hades. "You have no allegiance to Imada. And till now, no reason for me to imprison you. However breaking and entering might count against you."

"Zeus assigned you to the depths for a reason, brother," Sara says. "You, like your new Gorgon friend here, are a snake. You've always been the scum beneath the earth. That's why you associate yourself with one. So make way and go crawl back in your hole. Let me have my nectar. I won't use it. I simply intend to make sure no one else gets it. Mostly, my deranged daughter."

"Deranged?" asks Cora, laughing. "Look what you're doing."

"Cora," says Hades, cocking his head to her, "Doesn't that scepter belong to the Ambrosia family? Didn't I gift it to your grandmother, Harmonia, so many millennia ago? And you've said many times that you are the daughter of Nephrea Ambrosia, not the daughter of this old crone. The gods no longer lay claim to that staff."

"Right." Cora nods.

"Perhaps you should take possession of it from this imposter?"

The room explodes in light. I have to shield my eyes. They were getting accustomed to darkness. But I can still smell. My nose watches what looks almost like an illusion, it happens so fast. Sara moves like a blur to the other side of the room, avoiding the lightning strike. Then it's dark as quickly as it was bright. But my eyes are burning from the lightning bolt. Fire erupts. The window where Sara was standing is now a gaping hole. The lightning strike was likely caused by Cora's magic. But my living room has caught on fire. The flames are fighting against the rain pouring in through a gaping hole that was once my living room wall.

Hades rushes Sara. He wrestles her until they're both hurled through a wall by my entryway. Cora somehow manages to grab the scepter in the melee and toss it to me. It's thrown too high, but my snakes catch it by the ceiling. Then Cora's grabbing Sara's arm. Hades grabs for Sara's other arm. They're trying to pin her down to capture her, but Sara's too strong. She hurls both of them from her. Then she bursts through my front door.

We're outside. There's a crack or two from a rifle, but the gunshots from the soldiers are scant. I think the army outside doesn't want to shoot Cora and Hades and, anyway, the three of them are moving so fast that they're barely trackable by the human eye—barely even discernable by my monster nose.

There's a crack of thunder amidst the rain again. A lightning bolt misses Sara by just an inch. Or maybe it hits her, because she falls, dazed. Then the rain pours down even harder, limiting the view and smell. But I catch Hades grabbing Sara. She flicks her extended wrist in his direction and he's hurled across my front yard into one of my trees.

Sara rushes him, but there's another explosion of light. The tree bursts into flames. Sara evaded the lightning bolt again. But now she's rolling on the ground with Cora.

Another flash of light. Then another. One lightning bolt after another comes down, with cracks of thunder. Cora grabs hold of her mother and tosses her all the way across the street, and Sara smashes into a parked car.

Sara recovers, oddly lifting her arms high above her head.

The rain stops. It changes to icy hail. Then snow falls. It's at least fifty degrees colder in seconds. I feel as if I just walked into a freezer. The snow begins with flurries, then plummets down. And Cora's lightning bolts finally stop brightening my yard. Only the sound of thunder appears in the dark night sky.

Snow falls in blankets, covering my house, Hades, and Cora. Oddly, in less than a minute, Hades and Cora are buried.

Somehow, I escape the ice and snow and make a run for it across the street to help Asher and Sandra. There, soldiers are struggling to find shelter from the ice and wind. And the blizzard has kicked up so much wind that the SUVs are sliding across the road. One has even flipped over.

I hurdle over a tree sliding in front of me as I cross the road. Then I find Ash and Sandra under a couple feet of snow. I plop down and dig all the ice off them. They're unconscious under the ice. I brush all the snow from their bodies. Then I notice Engel's nowhere to be found.

"Where's the jar!" Sara storms. *"Where is it, Gorgon!"*

I turn back to the road and find Sara walking headlong through the blizzard. Her bright, fiery red eyes shine like flashlights as she heads right at me. One soldier, dug into the snow, manages to shoot her shoulder, but unlike me, the goddess keeps walking as if she isn't even dazed.

She grabs me and throws me off Asher and Sandra. Then she holds me up in the air by my neck. My feet leave the ground as she strangles me and I struggle to breathe.

"Where is it, serpent! Tell me now! My brother and daughter are frozen in ice, but not for long. Hurry quick! If they wake up, I'll kill your friends!"

Her gaze at Ash and Sandra turns their bodies red in the

light of her fiery eyes. Still holding me by the neck, she plows her other hand down in the snow, reaching for either Asher or Sandra. I squirm and cut at her with my claws. It's no use. I can't break free. I even claw her arm and draw some blood, but it seems to not even affect her.

She grabs Sandra's arm. Sandra awakens and screams, gazing into her fiery demon eyes.

"I'll kill this woman!" cries Sara. "Where is the jar, Guardian? Tell me right now or I'll break this girl."

Tell her, Gorgi. Help Sandra!

"It's... It's." I cough, struggling to breathe. Everything turns black for a moment. Then I open my eyes, bathing her face in green light. She loosens her grip. I fall on my knees before her. "The roof." I gasp for air again. "It's between... tiles under the chimney."

Sara smiles wickedly.

She lets go of Sandra's and my necks and races like a blur, at incredible speed, to the house. I squint and make out her figure scaling the columns on my deck like a monkey with only three large leaps. Amidst the pounding ice and wind, she digs the ice around my chimney. She starts hurling tiles off my roof. It's not hard to find. I see her lift a crystal jar.

The blizzard becomes intolerable. I'm back to covering Ash and Sandra, trying to warm them. They're not moving. I think they're frozen solid. Is that what happened to Cora and Hades?

But why am I not frozen?

She needed you to tell her where the jar was.

But what about now?

It's so cold...

11

FORECAST CALLS FOR SNOW

IT'S SNOWING IN SUNLAND. YEAH, JUST WHEN I THOUGHT I'VE seen everything—like a bay in Italy freezing into an ice rink —my Florida home and neighborhood is covered in a blanket of snow. But it stopped. It's become quiet. The clouds are gone and I can see the stars. The wind even stopped blowing. Red and blue lights are reflected all over the ice from the ambulances and police cars now lining the streets. The soldiers are gone too. And so are the gods. Good riddance. They destroyed everything.

I blacked out. I don't know what happened after Sara stole the jar. I found myself being revived by a paramedic next to Ash and Sandra. We literally froze. So did Cora and Hades, I think. That's how Sara must have stopped them.

Now, Sandra, Asher, and I are just sitting in these thick dark blue blankets, shivering like crazy, feeling miserable on the floor of the back of an ambulance. The back door is wide open. At first, they shut it to keep us warm. Now, with how weird the weather is, they opened it to warm the inside of the ambulance. Yeah, weird. My hair's turned long and wet, but thin. I guess everything's becoming "normal"—except the snow. Though it's getting hot outside, there's still snow everywhere. And we're all totally in shock. Not just Sandra this time.

All our relics are gone, Gorgi! They're gone!

I know. I know.

Asher rubs my back as if reading my mind. He flashes me a forlorn grin. I think it's the first time he's moved in the last ten minutes.

"I'm going to see if I can get my landlord to open up my new apartment early for me tomorrow night," says Sandra. Ash throws her a real nasty look. "Sorry," Sandra says quietly, looking at me. Then she looks down at the floor. "Sorry," she says, shaking her head.

"You guys feeling all right?" asks a tall paramedic in a blue EMS jumpsuit. Somehow, Orcus did his magic and all the cops and EMS professionals think the house was simply on fire from lightning. Not sure he'll be as lucky at explaining the snow. "You warming up?"

"Yes," Ash says with a nod. "Thank you."

"The fire that hit your house is out, ma'am," he continues. "But I wouldn't go inside. It's dangerous. The roof could cave in and there's actual holes in the walls. The lightning storm was that bad. And, well, there's not much left inside."

Sure. I know. Thunder and lightning breaking down all the walls of my house. Now snow. Just another day in Sunland, Florida.

My gaze wanders to Cora's black sports car, parked in front of my house. The McLaren is still completely covered in a blanket of white ice.

Asher leans over when the paramedic leaves and says, "You okay?"

"No, Ash. I'm not okay. All my relics..."

"God, Gorgi," he says, hugging me. "I'm so sorry."

I nod. But I don't cry.

I know you want to cry, Medusa, but...I won't. It won't change anything.

I hate her.

Sandra?

No, the gods. And...

"Mind telling me why it was snowing?" asks Ash.

"Do you know why Cora's mother, her foster mother, Nephrea, rushed down into the Underworld to save her thousands of years ago?"

"You told me it was to save Cora?"

"No. I mean, yes, but that wasn't all. Cora told me her real mother, Sara, the goddess Demeter, iced the entire planet when Cora was abducted. Sara threatened to keep the world under ice unless her brother, Zeus, released Cora from the Underworld. She managed to create famine and death in the ancient world, terrible destruction starving thousands until Nephrea agreed to risk her life in search of Cora. See, Cora can control rain, and her mother, Sara, can freeze things. That's how Sara stopped them. And that's how she stopped Cora from hitting her with lightning. Demeter is a frigid cold bitch."

Ash nods.

"And I think she got the scepter." I heave a sigh. "I lost it again."

"You lost the scepter?"

"Just like I lost the jar," I say with a shrug and a sigh. "I hate to say it, Ash, but Hades is right. I don't make much of a guardian of anything."

"This wasn't about guarding things, Gorge," Ash says. "It was about protecting Sandra and Engel."

Sandra looks up and flashes me a smile.

The paramedic shouts back from the front of the ambulance. "Take them to Sunland ER."

"We can't go until the roads are cleared," says the person

in the driver's seat. "I've never seen anything like this in my life."

I smell three kids laughing and plowing through ice, throwing snowballs at each other. And another guy, further down the street, is running and sliding on the icy sidewalk. The kids are already having fun even though the sun hasn't risen yet. It doesn't snow in Florida very often, you know.

Guardian.

What? Wait, is that you?

Only Engel calls you Guardian, Gorgi.

I lift my head and sniff. I sniff all over my front yard and backyard. I see a green schematic map of my whole property. Then I do what I really don't want to do. I sniff inside my ransacked house. I search the living room and bedroom, which is just a hollowed-out shell of what my place used to be. It's so awful.

Guardian, I have the jar.

It is Engel's voice. But where is his voice coming from?

I jump out of the ambulance and look all around me.

"What's the matter, Gorgi?" asks Ash.

"When I was in the house fighting Sara, was Engel with you two?"

Ash shakes his head. Sandra shakes her head too.

I put a finger to my chin. Then I peek under the ambulance.

Guardian, Demeter doesn't have the jar, I do. If you can hear me... I can return it to you.

"Where are you, Engel?" I ask out loud. Of course, judging from how far away his words seem, he can't hear me.

"Gorgi, you're still shivering," Ash says. "Just stay here."

Nah. I've felt worse. I hand my blanket to Ash and rush back to my house.

12

MY RELICS

I'm standing in my entryway. The power's out, obviously, and it's dark. But dawn is starting to creep through the cracks and holes in my broken walls.

My place is a complete wreck. Like, I mean, unrecognizable ruins. Icicles have formed like stalactites hanging from my ceiling. The kitchen counter and table are missing. Turning to my living room, I see the sofa's been gutted, with pieces of foam along wood and wet fabric. Rocks and dust have replaced the fireplace. There are holes in the walls the size of doors. And nearly every glass window is shattered or missing. I have the choice to walk down the hallway to my bedroom or just walk through one of the holes in the walls. Yeah. I mean, my place is gutted. It's all fucking gone.

Well, I'm not going to cry about it. My other half is doing enough sobbing as is... See, she's not saying anything. Yoohoo, Medusa? You there?

Nope. See.

"Engel?" I ask near my dining room table. "Engel. Where are you?"

"Here, Guardian."

I whip my head around, following the snakes on my head. My vipers are pointing behind me, toward my front door. That's where Engel's standing. I think he was standing behind the door when I walked in. How did I not detect him?

And yet, he was not saying "I'm over here" when he said "here." He meant "here," as in take the wine bottle in his outstretched hands. His body is shaking. Mine too. I don't think it's fear. I don't think this little guy fears a thing, but it's freezing in my house.

I snatch the bottle from his hands. Then I use my eyes, now glowing emerald, to inspect the contents. In the bottom is a dark fluid. It appears auburn or black under my shiny green eyes. Is it nectar? In a wine bottle?

"This isn't the jar," I say.

"Sì. While you and your friends fought each other, I made for the roof. I figured she'd get it from you eventually. If not, I'd simply swap the contents back again. But I had seen you hide the jar on the roof before. So I took a bottle of wine and swapped the contents. I suppose some of the stuff is wine now. I mean, the nectar is red like red wine. And apparently they look enough alike to fool Demeter. She fell for it and ran. Then I saw Hades and Cora awaken from their ice slumber and chase her."

"But this bottle is glass. It can be shattered."

"Sì. We no longer have an enchanted crystal jar. That's the only problem with the exchange. It can break. But we have the nectar inside it." The little man looks around the house. "The jar's gone, just like your house. I'm so sorry for what's happened, Guardian. What happened here is inexcusable. It's yet another act of violence by the infernal Olympian gods. Ever since I've met you, I've watched you help others. You didn't deserve this."

I fall on my knees and swoop the man in my arms. I feel

him jerk in surprise. "You're wonderful, Engel! You're the real guardian, not me."

He laughs. Then he shakes his head.

"I told you before that *you* are The Guardian. Every action I've witnessed since I met you involved guarding people."

"Not the scepter and jar."

"But you tried, Medusa. And your friends were more valuable to you. That makes you more worthy of holding this treasure than anyone else. It's something that the wretched gods can't do."

I smell another intruder and jump up. Then I lift my head and sniff. I don't need to. I hear footsteps on the carpet. It's coming from my bedroom. It would be easy enough for anyone to enter. There are holes throughout my walls. Then I recognize her scent. I'd recognize her anywhere.

"Arachne!"

"Buondì, Medusa," she says, walking into my arms. Her accent, like Engel's, is a welcoming, lovely Italian. "Buondì."

"You're here?"

She nods with a wry smile.

I can't believe she's here. But she is. Her eyes are multiple small black dots, she's bald, and she's wearing a black leather dress. But even her permanent spidery transformation is lovely. Even as a spider, Arachne is a lovely woman.

"I thought you were still in Italy."

Arachne laughs and shakes her head. "I'm here with Engel. We're friends and we stay together. But it seems like all our trouble is with you now. I'm so sorry. I knew the jar should go to you, but I never would have thought all this would happen because of it." She looks around the house and shakes her head. She takes me in her arms again. "Scusa. It is so wrong what they did to you. Scusa. So wrong."

She hugs me and, in her arms, I finally let a few tears go. It's the first time. All for my relics. Not the house. The house can be replaced. My relics are gone forever.

I move gently from her arms. I shake my head and wipe my tears. I feel so miserable, but being in her arms helped.

But then I'm reminded of her den in Portofino being destroyed a few months ago. I think of how the destruction of her home was different. The bombs not only destroyed her home; they destroyed her family of spiders. The destruction of my home didn't destroy family, only things. As important as my relics are, they were still only things.

So I say, shaking my head, "Oh, Arachne, my things were just mementos. I have people I love, like you."

"Bene," Arachne says with a sad smile. Tears run from her eyes too. She runs her hand along my hair. "Bene. You understand. Unlike them."

"That is why the scepter and nectar belong to you now, Guardian," Engel says.

Arachne reaches under his shirt and pulls out a golden rod. It's the Scepter of Azure. She hands it to me, and I take the golden rod into my hands.

"How did you get this?"

"Same as the jar," Engel says with a shrug. "You all were fighting so I just grabbed it before I got the jar."

"He's incredible," I say to Arachne.

"Sì," says Arachne. "Engel è molto speciale. He reminds me of you, Medusa. While you protect the scepter and jar, I protect Engel." Then she loses her smile. And she says, "But we must go. We can't be found. This time, there's no time to spend with you, Medusa. I'd invite you to come with us, but I know you won't join us."

I shake my head. Sure I'm a recluse, but I can't spend centuries in underwater caves or running. "If Imada detects our presence, they'll follow us and find us. You must tell no one that you saw us. Don't tell anyone about your possession of the nectar and scepter either."

"But what about Cora?"

"Especially Persephone," says Engel. Then he looks up at Arachne.

Arachne nods. She lays a hand on my shoulder. "Engel and I think you should leave them, Medusa." She hangs her head. "We...we've spoken many times before of this. But look." She extends an arm, gesturing at my home. "Tua casa. Persephone and you like each other, but the goddess is endangering Asher, all your friends, et la famiglia. Guarda. Guarda, Guardian. Witness everything Cora has done to you."

"She didn't. Sara did."

"All this continues if you stay with her, Medusa," Engel says. "Persephone will never change. After Nephrea and I escaped the Underworld, Nephrea said this to me. But even I didn't have the heart to tell Persephone. I know how much Persephone loved Nephrea, but Nephrea knew her daughter Cora's heart. Persephone will only destroy. You must leave her and the gods. Last night they destroyed your things. Tomorrow it will be those you love."

"But this was because of Sara. She's not Imada or on Cora's side."

"Engel and I take no side with any god, Medusa," snaps Arachne, angry for the first time. "I came here for you. We three are not gods. I tried to stop all the destruction of your home, but I was too late to stop Demeter. I failed. For that, I'm sorry. I feel responsible because I sent Engel to give you the jar."

"No, Arachne, it's not—"

Arachne shakes her head and raises her hand. "But I didn't fail in gifting the jar and scepter to the right person. The gods must never have it. And never know where it's hidden. If you stubbornly insist on still speaking with them, I ask that you never tell them you recovered them."

"You have to listen to us," Engel insists. "Leave Persephone. All she will do is hurt you. It's because of them, I tell you. Just like our den. It's not Imada, it's Hades and Cora. It is all the Olympian gods. We, all three of us, are not gods. You must turn from them, Guardian. Just as we do."

"We have to go, Medusa," Arachne says. She embraces me again. "I am so sorry."

"Thank you, Arachne."

"Will you guard the nectar, Guardian?" asks Engel.

I nod.

"Goodbye, Medusa," Engel says. "I served many Ambrosia queens for centuries. Never was I forced to follow the Amazon nymphs, but I followed them out of my respect and love for them. And I tell you, Arachne is right about you. You are like their queens."

"Till next time, old friend," Arachne says with a smile and nod.

Arachne then takes Engel's hand. They walk down the hallway to my bedroom. From the smell, I can see a hole big enough for them to fit through that leads to my backyard. And then I'm left alone. I'm left alone in a shell of what was once my house.

I hear dripping water. That's ice melting. And then I see brighter light. It's coming from holes in the walls. The sun must have risen. And that brings up a problem I haven't even worked out yet. Now I'm homeless. And I've got snakes in my hair that come out during daylight. Where am I going to go?

With Asher.

Hi, Medusa. I thought you were gone.

Don't talk about it.

Well, I don't like Ash's roommate. I think I dislike Dale more than Sandra.

I don't mind Sandra so much.

Yeah, I remember you actually cared about her when Sara almost killed her.

She's not so bad.

My cellphone buzzes. I look down at the bright screen of my cracked cellphone. The contact reads *Cora*. She messaged: "My mother doesn't have the nectar. It's replaced in the jar. Brilliant! Where'd you hide it?"

THE END

Gorgiana and Cora continue their Greek mythological mayhem in the 21st century in "The Furies Series":

- MY EVIL EYE
- THE GUARDIAN
- NECTAR OF AMBROSIA
- CORA

PARTING WORDS

What did you think of *Nectar of Ambrosia*? By placing a book review, you can inform others of your thoughts and help spread the word about my book.

Want more? Periodically I like to send news regarding current or new projects. If you'd like to be privy, I encourage you to sign up to my email newsletter. Your information will remain private and you can cancel any time.

Sign up at www.alhawke.com or scan the following QR code:

ALSO BY A.L. HAWKE

URBAN FANTASY ROMANCE

- MY EVIL EYE
- THE GUARDIAN
- CORA

PARANORMAL ROMANCE

- ALONDRA
- BROOMSTICK
- WINDSTORM
- THE HAWTHORNE WITCH

GHOST & ANGEL ROMANCE

- SHADES
- PHANTOM MASQUERADE

FANTASY: THE AZURE SERIES TRILOGY

- CORA: RISE OF THE FALLEN GODDESS
- AZURE BLUE
- CORAL RED

SCIENCE FICTION

- THE CANDY SAVANT DUOLOGY

Books available at https://alhawke.com/books

MY EVIL EYE

Don't look at me. Just don't.

My name's Gorgiana. For decades, I've lived a happy, simple life, shelving books at Sunland University's library in Florida. But my peace ended when I witnessed an assault, bringing back horrors from my past. Or course, I took care of him. His body's no longer whole. But that revealed my location.

I asked for help from my best friend, Cora, the goddess Persephone, and everything turned out just peachy. More than peachy. I met this real hot guy named Ash that same night. Later he took me out to a nightclub by the beach—next, a movie. All was well, until some thug stuck a gun in my boyfriend's back. But I took care of him. He's in pieces now too. But it all puts Medusa in a heap of trouble.

See, my name's Medusa. Yeah, I'm that monster with the snakes in my hair. I warned you not to look.

Book I in The Furies Series.

THE GUARDIAN

Medusa vacays on the Italian Riviera to stop her best friend from destroying the world.

I'm staying off the coast on the Italian Riviera in Portofino. Have you ever been? It's this gorgeous bay surrounded by rectangular red and yellow pastel buildings with swanky shops, restaurants and gorge trails.

Well, I don't want to be here. And I *really* didn't want my lover to join me. See, I came to protect my friend. The ancient Greek gods of Olympus claim Arachne holds the Scepter of Azure. The Scepter is a weapon that can freeze an entire city. Well, I don't really care about the Scepter, I care about my friend. Of course, Arachne can hold her own. Don't ever underestimate animals like spiders—or snakes, like me, for that matter.

The Guardian is a short story.

Medusa returns from *My Evil Eye* in this vacation urban fantasy novella. Although *The Guardian* is chronologically Book II in the Furies series, this book is a distinctive stand-alone that was written to be enjoyed without having read the first novel, *My Evil Eye*.

Book II in The Furies Series.

NECTAR OF AMBROSIA

Medusa tries her hand at wedding planner

as the gods tear apart her city.

My boyfriend's sister, Sandra, is getting married and she's asked for my help. Well, I've seen plenty of weddings over the centuries, so I've got some cool ideas. Only thing is, Sandra and I don't get along.

But that's hardly the worst of it. Apparently there's this dwarf with blue skin roaming around Sunland University looking for me so that he can give me Pandora's Jar. Pandora's Jar contains the last drops of nectar, an elixir that can magically turn any mortal immortal. And if you've ever met Persephone's infernal family, they've lived for thousands of years and become a pretty lonely bunch. Because they're awful people.

Well, I don't want to have anything to do with protecting their jar. I'd rather plan Sandra's wedding. Unless they threaten my home. If they do that, Medusa's gonna tear them into little pieces.

Medusa's back home in Florida in this urban fantasy. But there's a storm brewing. Although *Nectar of Ambrosia* is chronologically Book III, this book is a stand-alone that was written to be enjoyed without having read the first novel, *My Evil Eye*.

Book III in The Furies Series.

CORA

Cora has it all, but she doesn't have a man.

They keep dying on her.

She is the immortal Greek goddess Persephone, drinking and reveling in a Malibu beach house in the twenty-first century. But no matter her wild antics or psychotherapy, nothing can ease the pain over her latest husband's murder. Except perhaps the prudish but handsome Mr. Gabriel Cartwright.

Gabe is a young East Coast realtor who's hired to transfer her things to her new home in Toronto. Cora likes him. He has such a kind and sweet heart. But her lover holds secrets. He is a member of a nymph race that Imada, an ancient order of gods, has been hunting to extinction; a race Persephone has fought millennia to protect. That's why she hired him. She wants to be close to him. She wants to care for him. Only Imada cares for Gabriel too—they want him dead.

Cora will protect her man or tear Imada apart trying.

A novel from The Furies Series.

EXCERPT FROM MY EVIL EYE

THE FOLLOWING EXCERPT IS FROM "CHAPTER 1 - FUGU TIME" IN MY EVIL EYE, FROM THE FURIES SERIES BY A.L. HAWKE

They always look at me funny. Whenever I roll my cart down the aisles shelving books, readjusting my glasses over my nose, or even just typing on the computer, boys look at me weird. Somehow they know I don't quite fit in. I know. I don't. But you know, to monsters, it's the normal people that are the weirdos.

There's one now. Look at him. He's just leaning against a wall with his sweaty armpit over the nose of a poor blonde in a cute sky-blue university sweater who's trying to study. She doesn't look like the type that normally studies—neither does the jock—but this is dead week, when students actually have to. She's trying to humor him by looking up and smiling, but I know she really wants him to leave her alone.

Don't look at him. Forget about him.

I shake my head and shelve a heavy textbook.

I'm in the main hall of Sunland University's library. It's a grand retro-nineteenth-century hall with loads of walnut columns and bookshelves and a vaulted dome ceiling. On one side is a waterfall. Yeah, an actual waterfall. And they have plants surrounding it, which I love because with the lighting and foliage, it makes me feel I'm outdoors and it's daytime. I like to read here late at night when I finish work early. On the other side of the hall is a bunch of offices behind windowed walls. Everything's lit by modern-looking chandeliers.

Shit, there's another creep bugging the girl. This ape won't stop fucking slapping her shoulder. I always perk up when guys act like this. I was violated in Sarpedon eons ago, you know. Even a little playing around is *not okay.*

Hey, don't look at me. Don't do that!

What a bunch of assholes.

Calm down, Gorgi.

Well... Don't fucking look at me!

He turns. Then he leans over and whispers something to her. I move my wigglies back from my ear to snoop.

"Come on. You want the stuff or not?"

"Give it to me or just leave me alone, Carl."

The guy standing over her looks right at me.

Keep your eyes off me!

My gaze is deadly, you know. It's like Fugu. Do you know what Fugu is? Fugu in Japanese translates to "fortune." It's the puffer fish. The puffer fish is a delicacy that tastes wonderful but, if not prepared just right, the poison doesn't give you good fortune. I've tried Fugu. It's not *that* great, even when prepared right. I've had it prepared wrong too. (It tastes the same, by the way.) Anyway, my eyes are like Fugu. They lure you in, entice you, but if you enjoy too much...bye, bye. Hey, what a coincidence—I'm shelving a book on Japanese cuisine.

"Excuse me?" Someone is tapping on my shoulder.

I whirl around. Being an A+ apex predator, it's rare that someone sneaks up on me, but I was distracted by the jerks.

"Can you help me with my book search?" he asks.

It's this tall guy with wavy golden hair thrown to the side. His face is a little sunburnt. He's wearing a button-down and baggy pants. He's got broad shoulders and strong arms. He's grinning. And he's cut and he's, *uh, hmm,* hot.

Oops. He opens his eyes wide. Did he see my cursed eyes? No, he's looking over at those two assholes laughing at the girl.

"I—" He coughs. "I figured you work here?"

"I do," I say, looking down at the floor.

"Can you help me? I'm in this Western Civ class, and the professor's asking for us to check out a book. I think she thinks it's like an inside joke. I mean, who checks out books at a library anymore when there's the web? No one. It's kinda stupid."

"There's lots of stuff in books you can't find online."

"Oh," he says, looking flustered. "Of course, *a librarian* would say that." He stops talking. I think it's because I'm staring at the ground.

Yep, he leans down to look into my eyes. I turn away.

"Are you okay?" he asks.

I nod. But I don't look at him. I want to. I really do. I already caught a glimpse of his strong jawline, five o'clock shadow, perfect teeth, and kind smile.

"I was just saying we could google it," he continues, rubbing his neck. "But the professor wants us to use the library. I've seen you working here before. You're one of the librarians. Right?"

"Yes."

He smiles again. He has such a cute smile. It's telling me he's not really here to search for books, you know.

Shit, did he catch a glimpse of my Fugu? Is that it? I wear these thick spectacles with special lenses to hide my golden gems, but they're not perfect. If a guy gazes straight into my eyes, it's Fugu time. Particularly if my gold gems turn green.

Sometimes somebody catches a glimpse from the side. Many years ago, I went to an optician to fit me with trick glasses that would be clear for me but blurry straight on for wandering eyes. I've tried lots of ways to hide my cursed eyes. Opaque shades work too, but Charlie, he's my boss, wouldn't take kindly to his librarians wearing sunglasses at work.

"Can you help me?" Oh yeah, the blond guy's still talking to me.

He follows me down three steps into another part of the library I love, with the gorgeous fountain I was talking about. The fountain has lovely trickling water. It's made of white stone and, I mean, it's not the Trevi Fountain, more of a tacky bozzetto, but I absolutely adore it. It was here decades ago when I applied for the job. I think it's what sold me. And tables circle the fountain, with computers where you can search for stuff. Students also sit on the three steps, but they're nearly always empty when I work here at night.

I sit down in front of a large antique monitor.

"What would you like to search for?" My eyes are focused on the screen.

His sunburnt hand is beside mine. Mine, peeping out from my ugly thick furry brown sweater, hovering over the keyboard, is tanned, always the same olive color, sun exposure or not. I don't burn—or, when I do, it just goes back to the same color. He has strong hands. Cute, nicely groomed strong man hands.

"Genghis Khan," he says, leaning over my shoulder.

"Genghis Khan," I say, typing fast. "This is similar to a google search. It's easy. You just type your word. You get the location here and the ISBN. Get it?"

"What's an ISBN?"

"It's an identifier. All books have them."

I feel tingles sitting near him. And I hear his heart jump a little. And his scent, his essence is... *like ...*

"Excuse me for not knowing what an ISBN is," he quips.

"Well..." I brush my bangs from my eyes with a smile. "Once you find the location, you can look for it by subject. We use the Library of Congress classification system here, not the Dewey Decimal. See, this shows a map of our library and where each category of books is shelved. And here's a call number for a book. Easy, right?"

"Easy for you."

He is staring at my profile. I turn a little so he doesn't see my eyes.

"You really like this stuff, don't you?" he asks.

"I love books."

"*Come on!*" snaps one of the meatheads in a forced whisper. I had totally forgotten about them. "*Hand it over or forget the whole thing.*"

"*Just leave her alone, Carl.*"

"*Let me go. Here's the money.*"

Let me go?!

I look up. I can't see anything past the fountain, but I can smell them. With my nose, I sense a hand yanking his prey's arm. My wigglies fight to break out from their cage in my hair. I press down on my bun. Then I glance back at the boy beside me. He's none the wiser, but he's squinting at me.

"Genghis Khan?" he asks, raising his brow.

"Oh." I start typing fast again. "Here's a directory of over twenty books on the subject. Just go to the third floor and find this section." I tap the screen. "I'll print out a list of call numbers for your report."

I quickly get up, looking toward the commotion.

"Can you show me the location upstairs?"

"What?" I ask, turning back to him with a laugh. "It's easy."

"Easy for you."

"Let me go! Where are you taking me!"

That fucker is tugging her arm! Can you believe this? That fucking dick is pulling her! I sense the whole building like a green schemata in my mind. And the angrier I get the clearer the image becomes.

I've had enough. I rush up the steps from the fountain back up to the main hall.

"Oh...well, thanks," blurts the student.

"Let me go, Carl!"

Let me go?!

I hear the struggle through the walls. They've left the main hall. No one else has any idea this commotion is going on. The struggle isn't loud; it's more like forced whispers. But the girl's panic rings in my ears.

When I was in Sarpedon, I was tricked by the slick, sugary tongue of Poseidon. And the horror began when the god grabbed my wrist. It's been thousands of years, but as the girl is dragged, I feel her pain as if he's dragging me by the arm.

I need to calm down. I can't change in front of these kids.

But he touched her. He's forcing her!

My hair is aching to escape its hair tie. My incisors are digging into my lower lip. I grasp my hands tightly, trying to distract myself, telling myself not to change—not to do that in front of all these students. But I want to hurt him.

I hear a body being thrown against a wall. It's a faint sound. My eyes are burning like green flashlights through my spectacles. Bright emerald. I shade my eyes as I break out into a run.

I hear a shirt tear. And she cries out as he twists her arm again.

Oh, you going to do that? Huh? Okay, you know what I'm

going to do? I'm going to dislocate your wrist, pull your hand from its socket, and stuff it down your motherfucking throat!

I rush down a hallway that connects the library to a nearby lecture building. A girl by the library exit, who's standing by a table reading, stares up at me as I sprint past her. Her human ears probably don't hear the struggle.

Everything turns dark and empty as I enter the corridor into the lecture hall. I follow their scent into another hallway. Then one more turn. And then...

I throw open the door to a boy's bathroom. It's empty. But there's movement in one of the stalls. I rush over and pull at the stall door. It's locked. I easily break the metal door open.

The asshole has the girl bent over facing the toilet. He doesn't even stop groping her—he's locked in predatory mode. Her shirt is torn, revealing bare breasts, and he's dropped his pants. He looks over his shoulder. Actually, they both do.

What a sight I must be. I'm not covering my green eyes anymore. Their bodies are illuminated in green light.

"Go," I say to the girl. "Get out of here."

The girl nods, clutching her torn shirt over her chest. She runs past me to the exit in tears. I turn to the creep. He's such a pompous ass that he faces me, still bathed in green light, with his cock wagging.

I'm feeling pain in my wrist. Is it my ancient memory of Greece? Or is it my empathy for the girl?

She's gone. It's over. Just let him go.

Uh... Nuh-uh.

I smile lasciviously at the boy. I remove my ugly brown sweater. I take off my shirt and bra and lay them gently by the sink. I take my time getting naked in front of him. Let him relish my poison. He's frozen after seeing my eyes.

"Is this what you wanted?" I ask. I slowly back away. "A nude girl?"

He gazes at my body with wide eyes. He doesn't seem to care that I look like a demon from hell right now, with fangs, sharp fingernails, and green, glowing eyes. He wants a taste of my body. A taste of my delicious Fugu. And, boy, is he gonna get it.

His body, though frozen, trembles.

"Who are you?" he asks, struggling to move his mouth. "*The librarian?*"

"I'm the devil."

I walk up to his ear and lick it. Then I brush my palm along his bushy beard and brush my tits against his side. "You want to sin? Sin with me. I'm not innocent. I can show you a good time."

"Sure," he purrs.

I run my hand along his shirt. His hands are weak, so I help him lift it. Then my hand runs over the bulges of his huge pecs. I pull the pants, still bunched around his ankles, away from his feet. Now he's naked and dirty, just like the filthy motherfucker he is.

But I freeze for a moment. I clutch my head in my hand... What am I doing? The girl's gone. She's safe. I can just stop. Right?

NO! He was bending her over like a dog! You gonna let a man do that? After all that's happened to you?

I run my lips along his. Then I slowly wrap my fingers around his wrist. I twist. I could yank his hand right off with one more turn. Oh, it'd be so easy.

Cut it off and stuff it down his motherfucking throat!

No. I... I can't do that.

He winces and writhes as I twist. Then he shrieks. His body jerks to nurse his injured hand, but he can barely move.

"Why'd you do that?" he asks.

I giggle.

"What's your name?"

"Medusa."

My tongue comes out, forked like a snake's tongue, at the utterance of my ancient name. It licks his cheek and ear. But my long serpent tongue doesn't bother him the slightest bit. I reach back with my free hand, as I continue to stroke his cheek with the other, and finally free the bun from my head.

Oh, what a relief! As the bun unfolds, my black hair falls, freeing my friends, and the snakes thicken, slithering and slinking over my face. I take a deep breath as my beasties are let loose. Some of the black snakes run along his face. A couple even loop around his neck. I could choke and suffocate him. I've done it before. He's already too far gone to resist.

I should just snap his neck and be done with him.

No. Tease him. Make sure he's just conscious enough to feel the pain he brought her.

"You naughty, naughty boy," I whisper in his ear. I run my forked tongue along his ear. "How could you do that to an innocent girl?"

"Oh, she's not innocent," he says with a chuckle. My forked tongue enters his mouth and wraps around his tongue. I could constrict it and remove it.

Don't. Not yet. Play with him first.

I pull back from his lips, but it takes all my will to not pull out a chunk of his face.

"She was cheating on me," he says.

"Cheating on you? A virile young man? I don't believe it. So you were going to force a fuck?" At the word *fuck* his body shakes. "Because she deserved it?"

He chuckles nervously.

"Did she force the other boy to have sex too?"

"They met at a hazing," he says. His head is immobile. Only his mouth moves. "My friend met up with her after to study." I run my hand along his thick beard again. I hear his heart beating like crazy. "Next thing I knew I saw them screwing on my bed. So what I did was I planned this whole deal. I wanted to teach her a lesson and show her who her true boyfriend really is. My way. I figured the bathroom was private." He looks at my eyes, but I don't meet his gaze. There's enough green from my eyes in the room to entrance him. A little more and he wouldn't be able to move his mouth and finish his stupid excuse. "I guess... not so private."

"Touch my hair," I say. "Go on."

He lifts a shaky hand and runs his fingers along my hair. My vipers coil around them. Perhaps this would be enough? I can sever his fingers and leave him with a maimed hand? That would teach him a lesson, wouldn't it?

No. Kill him! Kill him!

"Well, you told me your story, my boy, why don't you let me tell you mine?" I cuddle his head on my breasts. "I'm going to give you quite a whopper."

"It was three thousand years ago. I worked in the temple of Athena. I was a priestess. Every day I toiled hard maintaining the goddess's great temple. I was a model priestess. Of course, I was a virgin. All those who worked the great temple of Athena were virgins. God forbid we were ever *fucked*..." His body shakes again. "Or defiled by horny boys."

I guide his hand along my side, and his fingers somehow manage to twitch along the crack of my ass. It makes me almost furious enough to finish him.

"I'm not done," I say, moving his hand from my butt. "Listen. One day, as I was out to gather water from the well, I was surprised by a voice. It was a stranger flattering me over my beauty. I had always known I was pretty. In fact, many think I am the most beautiful woman in the world. In fact, it was my beauty that drew so many other virgins to the temple. That was good for business, but bad for the goddess Athena's jealousy."

"Yes, you are hot," he mutters stupidly.

"Aha. The voice was Poseidon's. The god had seen me alone and came to me when I was vulnerable. The god grabbed my arm and tore off my sacred white robe and fucked me right there by the well. He fucked me like no man had ever fucked before. He was a mighty Olympian god, after all. He showed her who was boss, just like you were doing to that poor girl. Right?"

I laugh. There's really nothing funny about that. But it's too bad for him that he's too entranced to join me in my mirth. If he chuckled, that would be another reason for me to finish him off. Instead, the fucker finds the strength to lower his head and run his lips around my nipples.

Go ahead and suck. That's fugu too.

"Well, the very next morning, I ran. I ran from the temple because I had been defiled. My mere presence dirtied the sacred ground, and it was a grievous insult to the goddess Athena. I didn't get far. Athena came to me personally. She tripped me with Apollo's snakes."

I grab his cock. I pull a little, like I pulled his wrist. He winces. He leaves my tit and leans into my face, pressing his lips into mine. Apparently, he didn't notice my sharp fangs and slithering vipers.

"She turned me into one," I say with a shrug, between his kisses. "Ever since then, I've borne witness and left alone all sins. I turn my eyes from theft, adultery, even murder. But never, ever, ever do I avert my eyes from one sin. Do you happen to know what that sin is?"

He shakes his head.

"Rape," I say. "Rape is one thing I will never witness

again. When Poseidon pinned me, and the stars sent me no mercy, and when, instead of judging a god and punishing Poseidon, the gods turned on an innocent young girl and ruined her, I realized there is no one in this whole fucking world that cares about me. I have been discarded. Trash. For me, I'm done. But for another, no. I vowed to never, ever, ever, let that happen to another lady in my presence. Do I make myself clear?"

He nods with a smile, looking at me—full of desire—thinking somehow, weirdly, that I'm going to have sex with him. If someone were to walk in now and witness my fangs, my moving hair, and my glowing red eyes beside him, they might think this is funny. You do, right? But it really isn't amusing, is it?

He deserves punishment. Punish him.

The snakes in my hair move in a fury, hissing wildly. My eyes glow a brighter green, illuminating his whole face. When I am ready for the kill, I lose all attractiveness. But the boy seems too deep in his trance to notice.

"Now, tell me, what were you doing to that poor girl?"

He laughs. Then he gazes into my eyes and a shadow seems to fall over him. That's what I was waiting for. Realization. With my seduction, I've unleashed the lamia of his destruction. I am revenge. He loses all mirth. Well, like I said, there was nothing funny here. There never was. I reach down and grab his penis and...it's all over.

Look into the eyes of Medusa. Gaze into me as I ravish you. Keep your eyes on mine as your skin tears from your neck, shredding muscle and sinew, leaving your chest bloody and back bare. Your flesh I rip. Your arms and legs I tear. I dismember you into the heap of shit you are.

Still awake? Good. Feel more... Pain!

I should just leave him. She's gone and...

Take his hand and shove it down his throat!

His screams are muffled. His cries seem to be coming from so far away, as if in a faraway tunnel. At this point, I'm far into a trance myself.

And...

I black out. But, in my periphery, I watch a body fall to the floor—in pieces.

In the back of my mind, I recall screaming. Is it a memory or is it happening now? I'm not sure.

As I awaken further, I take a deep breath. I feel dizzy.

I walk to the bathroom mirror. Red is splashed on my face. I wash my face. As the crimson washes away and the snakes recede, my face is absolutely beautiful again. The prettiest face in the world. I arrange my hair back in a bun.

The metallic stench of his blood has taken the place of piss and shit and fills the bathroom. I walk to the door and realize I crushed the doorknob after the girl ran. Then, as I awaken more, I realize a bunch of people are banging on the door.

My God, what have I done? In my periphery, I see crimson flesh smeared and heaped against the white tile. There's only a mound of meat on the floor, no recognizable body.

There's a window on the other end of the bathroom. It's just big enough for us to slither through.

Go, Medusa! Run!

MEDUSA'S ADVENTURE CONTINUES IN MY EVIL EYE, THE FIRST BOOK IN FURIES

ACKNOWLEDGMENTS

I want to thank my beta readers Breonna H. and George B. for their insight, my line editor, Stephanie Marshall Ward, for polishing and my proofreader, Alexa, for perfecting. And, finally, my cover artist, Brosedesignz, for a fun and amazing work of art.

ABOUT THE AUTHOR

A.L. Hawke is the author of the bestselling Hawthorne University Witch series. The author lives in Southern California torching the midnight candle over lovers against a backdrop of machines, nymphs, magic, spice and mayhem. A.L. Hawke writes fantasy and romance spanning four thousand years, from pre-civilization to contemporary and beyond.

Visit A.L. Hawke at www.alhawke.com

Email: contact@alhawke.com